The Night Santa Forgot

by

Fabian Grant

Paperback edition first published in the United Kingdom in 2020 by aSys Publishing

Hardback edition first published in the United Kingdom in 2020 by aSys Publishing

eBook edition first published in the United Kingdom in 2020 by aSys Publishing

A CIP catalogue record for this book is available from the British Library.

ISBN: 978-1-913438-39-5

aSys Publishing 2020

http://www.asys-publishing.co.uk

RCatch Me If You Can
Instagram - mrfabiangrant
Twitter - @fabiangrant3
&
Don't forget to review on
Goodreads .com

# Contents

# CHAPTER 1

## The Origin of Christmas

Christmas is a time of sharing and giving unto others less fortunate than yourself. However, lately, the way you celebrate has dramatically changed. No more is it about giving presents and expressing kindness towards one another. Instead it has become about greed and personal gain. I for one hate Christmas with a serious passion: the mince pies, mistletoe and the roast turkey . . . I've had my fill. Nobody appreciates the real meaning and message behind it all and from where the whole story of Christmas originally started. Let me take you on a pleasant stroll down memory lane.

Long, long ago, in another time and place, way before the technological revolution took over and dare I say, ruined everything, life was a lot simpler. In a small well-known city called Bethlehem there lived a budding young couple named Mary and Joseph who were madly in love. I'm sure they had their own share of arguments and disagreements but overall (according to the books) seemed rather happy. Joseph worked as a carpenter, so we know he was good with his hands. Mary? Well she is a bit of a grey area for me; I'm not entirely sure what she did. Although back in that era the roles of female and males were more defined; men went out to work and the ladies kept house. Anyway, the story goes; Joseph, as happy as a pig in muck, popped the question. I'm unsure as to whether he got down on one knee. Anyway, Mary was overjoyed and replied instantly.

'Yes!' she exclaimed.

'You've made me the happiest man on earth love,' cried Joseph.

'Considering there's only handful of people living, it's not as big of a compliment as you might think.'

(I must state these conversations aren't accurate, I'm just going from what I was told.) The couple lived in modest accommodations. Then again, they all did; you've gotta remember these were the first civilised people. Mansions, armies and capitalism were yet to be established. Life must have been such a doddle; no laws, no rules, no money. People probably got away with murder. Actually, doesn't sound so brilliant, in hindsight. Nevertheless, the couple settled down in Nazareth and found themselves in a nice routine. Then one eventful day would alter the world as we know it. Mary was a very special lady and not just in the eyes of hubby Joseph; God himself also had a fondness for her. So roughly two millennia ago God sent his most trusted angel down with a message of monumental importance. Out of nowhere a dazzling light covered the room and angel Gabriel appeared to a frightened Mary.

'Please, there is absolutely nothing to fear,' spoke angel Gabriel.

Mary, intimidated, kneeled before the figure with her hands clasped. 'Who are you and what do you want with me?'

Angel Gabriel's halo grew brighter. 'I've travelled a long way to deliver sensational news, young lady.'

Mary's fears began to disappear as the angel's alluring smile engaged her intrigue. 'News regarding what exactly?'

'Mary, you will be blessed with a son.'

'How that's possible; I'm not married?' she said confused.

'The Lord has chosen you to give birth to his son, a boy who'll be named Jesus,' informed Gabriel.

The overwhelming news was almost too much for poor old Mary to take. Her head nearly exploded from the enormity of her responsibility.

You should feel honoured; God's entrusting you with the massive task of raising his offspring.'

'What if I refuse?' queried Mary.

Angel Gabriel giggled, amused by Mary's stubbornness. 'Do you really want me to tell God you said thanks, but no thanks? He created the world in seven or so days. Are you sure about your decision?'

'It's a lot to ask of me,' she whined.

Angel Gabriel saw her anxiety and realised how much he'd burdened her with. 'Listen, Mary, God doesn't give us tasks that we aren't capable of accomplishing. Is it difficult? Yes. Will it come with huge pressure? For sure. But with great talent comes great expectation.'

Mary thought about her stance; she loved The Lord and had faith in his plans. 'I am here to serve in his righteous name.'

'Splendid!'

'How will I know I'm preggers?'

'Oh, you'll know,' said Angel Gabriel disappearing.

'Wait, how do I explain this to Joseph? He'll have a million questions.'

As predicted, Joseph returned home from a long workday. Mary was very agitated, frowning as he sat down. Joseph seemed too tired to recognise his fiancée's dismay. It took a couple of days before Mary found the right opportunity to let Joseph in on her secret. One morning during breakfast— her hubby was always in good spirits when eating—she let it out.

'Joseph I've got some news that'll rock your mind,' said Mary.

'I pride myself on being prepared for everything,' he said, confident anything she threw at him he'd catch.

'I'm with child.'

4

Joseph dropped his spoon, utterly perplexed. He stared in astonishment. Mary's explanation didn't resolve his apprehension.

'How can that be? We haven't had . . . '

'I know it doesn't make sense. My reaction was identical to yours.'

Joseph adored Mary and over time came around to the whole notion of the Immaculate Conception. With the couple now committed to their duty of raising the Son of the Lord, Jesus' birth date loomed closer and closer. A burgeoning excitement began building in Mary and Joseph. However, before his arrival the duo were ordered to complete a registration in Bethlehem by the all-powerful Roman emperor Caesar Augustus. Bethlehem sits about 65 miles away from Nazareth and it's not like there were numerous modes of transport. Neither buses, coaches, taxis and most certainly Uber weren't invented. The heavily pregnant Mary and loyal Joseph supposedly rode to Bethlehem on a sturdy donkey. Once they reached Bethlehem, the couple hadn't thought ahead and sadly never booked a room. All the inns were already full. I'm guessing it must've been holiday season. The night drew in quickly; gleaming stars offered plenty of light as the temperature plummeted. The loved-up duo stumbled across an empty stable usually kept for animals. The stable was shoddily built; its weak wooden frame, feeble roof and rank smell disgusted the couple.

'I can't be having the Lord's child in a filthy stable,' complained Mary.

'We can't go any further and everywhere is rammed out, sweetheart. We'll just have to make do,' said Joseph rearranging bales of hay.

Fabian Grant

During the night Mary effortlessly gave birth to a little son. Joseph constructed a crib out of a manger using fresh hay and clothes. Baby Jesus glowed in the manger; his stunning form blessed both his parents. They couldn't keep their mitts off him.

'You shall be a leader of the people, my child,' said Mary, kissing her son.

Elsewhere, a few shepherds were observing their flock close to Bethlehem when suddenly an angel came forth.

'You should be the first to know today in Bethlehem a King is born. He has come to save your souls. Now go to him and spread the word,' demanded the Angel.

As instructed, the shepherd visited Jesus and told anyone who'd listen about the son of God.

The hype surrounding Jesus reached the furthest corners of earth.

'Have you seen him? He's adorable,' people spouted. Those lucky enough to stand within metres of Jesus fibbed about how they felt the Holy spirit enter their bodies. Mary expected a bit of buzz, yet nothing prepared her for what was to come, and not all of it positive.

In the east three wise men viewed a large glistening star, which to them signalled a new king was born. They immediately called in work sick and ventured to Bethlehem through searing heat and deserted land. While on their way to greet the new king one of the three wise blokes brought up a valuable point.

'Say, wise men, should we bring gifts?' he asked.

'What for? Like he'll remember,' replied the grumpiest wise man.

'Perhaps to get on his good side and stand out from the pack.'

6

'No need; you're being extra. He's the son of God. Anything we bring will come up short by the comparison.'

For three wise men they didn't half bicker over pointless stuff. What route to take, where to stop for lunch or whether the moon was just the sun with its rays turned down. 'Look, I'm not trying to compete with the almighty Lord, silly. I just feel a small token of our appreciation won't go amiss,' said wise man one, justifying his position.

'I don't see it as an unreasonable suggestion. It'll show our admiration, respect and love. Let's do it,' hollered the most joyous wise man.

So before meeting God's son they bought three rather unique presents.

The trio followed the extraordinary star until it hovered right above the house where Jesus rested.

One after the other they all knelt and quietly worshipped at his bedside. Mary unwrapped the three presents of gold, frankincense and myrrh. 'God bless you wise men,' she praised. Although Mary most likely thought he's a baby, why not baby clothes, a cot or dummy?

'He's the chosen one; it'd be sinful not to glorify him,' cheered a wise man.

See, this is true Christmas; three wise men selflessly offering gifts to a wonderful child. A baby boy who in the future would commit the greatest selfless act ever.

Now, we're bombarded with commercials selling toys, gadgets and expensive items.

After hearing my negative views, you'd assume I don't celebrate Christmas, but you'd be very wrong indeed. In fact, this year I've got the most important job of anyone else in the world.

# CHAPTER 2

## The Father of Christmas

Let's fast forward to the early 1800s. Christmas is no longer a small local holiday; it'd expanded into a major festival. Everybody loved the occasion. It gave you a chance to show real affection for the people who meant the most. Christmas still hadn't lost all its originality; many families told the story of the miracle birth and understood the meaning of giving. They sang carols, shared food and overall had a brilliant time in each other's presence. This worked for a sustained period of time. However, as life progressed, the world's population increased, altering the way Christmas was viewed. Families struggled to cope financially with purchasing presents. They'd scrimp and save all year round for one single day. At this rate Christmas as a whole was numbered, largely in parts to the burden and effort it took. Well off families kept Xmas alive for themselves, whilst poorer ones found it more troubling to do so. Each year certain kids suffered: trees got tinier, scattering needles across the carpet; gifts became fewer and gone were lavish meals replaced by whatever came cheap.

December 25th went through a bad dip in fortunes until one man galvanised the event. Nicholas Claus I was a fabulous toy maker who enjoyed nothing more than building a doll's house, mountain bike or train sets.

Business prospered throughout the Christmas period and orders came rushing in for specific items. Kids loved him for his ability and prompt delivery, and adults admired his quality products too.

'Every Christmas Nicholas Claus doesn't half take a weight off my mind,' said every parent in his region.

Whenever Christmas time rolled round, Nicholas Claus got this distinct feeling of remorse in his tummy. Yes, he brought positivity to a bunch of wealthy children, but neglected those without parents, which in his eyes weren't fair. At home two weeks prior to Christmas he battled his conscience, failing to fall asleep. Nicholas Claus' constant twisting and turning annoyed his Mrs Claus immensely.

'What's got you so agitated?'

'There's something wrong with my business model. I'm only looking after the rich and forgetting the needy,' Nicholas sadly stated.

You're making people happy and profiting in the process; what's so bad about that?'

'But Christmas hasn't got any ties to profit. It's a holiday of beauty. I just reckon all kids deserve presents, regardless of their parents' income, provided they are well-behaved.'

'So, what are you gonna do about it?'

'Give me time to think but bet your bottom dollar from this day forwards kids around the world well receive at least one gift under their tree,' promised Nicholas Claus. Mr Claus wouldn't let up on the idea that everyone should have a fantastic Christmas. Each morning he woke up before sunrise and strolled around the impoverished neighbourhoods, making a note of which kids lived where. As he passed by, he noticed sad children wearing the same tatty rags they had worn the day before. Youngsters played with sticks and rocks for fun; this resonated as Nick Claus' beautiful home was miles away from these ghastly conditions. That year Nick Claus worked his butt off, starting early and leaving his workshop late. His wife barely saw any of him as the intensity of his work schedule increased. Mr Claus finished his original list of presents then began producing additional toys for poorer kids. Originally Mr Claus had lovely flowing brown hair; he also never wore glasses and had a very slender figure. However, when you're busy-busy-busy things tend to deteriorate rapidly. His stomach grew larger from the free mince pies, cookies and eggnog he received. Due to the fact he now manufactured twice as many toys, his vision became progressively worse and blurred. As for his greying features, stress is a horrible consequence of success. The demands of being a generous gift giver accelerated the ageing process. Nick Claus remained determined to see his vision come true. He hired a few new workers to help him gift wrap and write out gift tags. By December 23rd Nicholas shut down his workshop, allowing his employees to spend time with their family. Some loyal workers stayed behind assisting him in locking up his business as there were various criminals lurking.

'Good luck sir; you've really put yourself out there,' said one of his workmen.

'How do you mean?' wondered Mr Claus.

'Well you can't just do this the one time. Good little boys and girls will expect presents every year till the end of time.'

Nicholas pulled down his metal shutters, realising that he'd just opened up a can of worms. 'My God, you're right. I'll have to work this hard each and every year.'

'Harder, even. Think when word gets out about your kindness to other villages and communities. You'll be swamped,' informed his worker.

A disgruntled Mr Claus sat on a park bench second guessing his career path. 'What the heck have I signed up for?'

His co-worker and good friend sat beside him in the bitter winter's night. 'Personally, I commend a man who sticks his neck out for something he feels passionate about. Whether you're right or wrong, you gotta follow through no matter what. It'd be miles worse if we let theses unlucky kids down.'

I'm exhausted though. To think this is just my first outing,' puffed Nicholas.

'Being the father of Christmas was never an overnight process nor guaranteed to prosper straight away.'

Nicholas looked at his friend slightly amused. 'The Father of Christmas didn't envision it like that.'

'Well you should. A hero requires a name and Father Christmas is suitable. You're a strong leader, a visionary and resolute all at once,' hollered the employer. Unscrewing his flask full of hot tea, he poured out two cups. 'Here is to Father Christmas, a guy destined to readdress the balance between the wealthy and deprived.'

'Cheers.' The two buddies swallowed the hot tea then drifted off to their separate homes.

The next day Mr Claus was satisfied he had sufficient presents to cater to all the poor children. He loaded up his sacks and stacked them on his cart. At first Mr Claus never used reindeer; they weren't suitable of traditional roads. Rudolph and his gang came later as he became more official. Early on Father Christmas transported goods using trustworthy steeds, as it displayed a level of class and importance. In the wee hours of Christmas Day Mr Claus made his very first delivery to a children's orphanage. Two small bells were attached the front of his cart; they rattled as he roamed up the street. Depressed little children ran towards the window in the hope something magical was taking place. It was a chillingly cold December morning, with five inches of snow settled on the stone road. Condensation rippled out the horse's mouths; they fluttered and flapped their lips. Father Christmas' outfit actually happened by sheer coincidence; Mrs Claus read the weather report and made sure her hubby wrapped up snugly. In a bargain department store in town his wife found an adorable red onesie with matching red hat. To prevent heat escaping the suit, Mrs Claus tightly fastened a belt around Father Christmas' waist. She demanded he wore it whilst distributing his items.

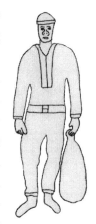

Another thing that I should mention is the whole theory of him sliding down a chimney; that's an urban legend, like Bigfoot or the Loch Ness Monster. Mr Claus had a quite novel approach to entering a home. He tapped the door knocker like a normal human. As he stood on the doorstep a huge amount of anxiety crept over him. When you put yourself out there, there's a significant possibility people won't receive you kindly.

The door tentatively opened; a curious lady eyed this stranger in a bright red onesie carrying a large sack. 'Hello? I'm sorry, we weren't expecting any parcels today.'

Father Christmas was at a loss for words. He didn't think in advance so there wasn't a dynamic script to read from. 'Greetings to all! I'm here to bring joy to all God's children.'

The orphanage worker stared on in utter confusion, wondering if a lunatic had landed on her door.

'Hey it's me, Mr Claus,' he said.

'You're not Mr Claus. He doesn't have a beard; he's always clean-shaven,' she informed, getting ready to slam the door.

'My week's been hectic and tiresome; shaving is the least of my priorities. Take a peek inside my sack; my toys are all stamped with Nicholas Claus' approval.'

The woman hesitantly opened up one of his presents; seeing Mr Claus signature carved into its base, she smiled. 'You had me worried for a second there. Please come in.'

Father Christmas patiently stood behind the door. The lady walked into the living room where several orphaned kids quietly played old style board games.

'Children, I've got a special surprise for you.'

The group of young kids squealed with heightened excitement. Their tiny faces were beaming.

Mr Claus' heart frantically throbbed again. He had his doubts.

'Boys and girls, I bring to you Father Christmas.'

The kids clapped loudly, focused on the door.

Mr Claus took a relaxing breath before waltzing in. As he strolled forward, Father Christmas stubbed his toe on a doorstop. 'Ho, ho, ho,' he groaned, and the catchphrase stuck forever. He played it off as part of his jolly routine. 'Greetings young ones, how are we this Christmas morning?

The usually giddy bunch remained silent, fixated on the bulging bag of presents.

Father Christmas realised he'd gotten their full attention and stalled building anticipation. 'Now as you may have gathered, I've overdone it this year, making far too many toys.' He paused tipping the sack upside down; hundreds of boxes littered the floor. 'Does anyone know someone who might be interested in free toys?'

A thunderous roaring response gave him his answer. The children hurried along aggressively, tearing the wrapping paper.

'You've made their year,' exclaimed the orphanage worker.

Father Christmas became rather emotional watching the pleasure those kids experienced. It dissolved all the hardship he'd put himself through. Mr Claus went on to make a record twenty-six deliveries to every home where a child was missing a present. That night Father Christmas made a startling declaration; no longer would he gift naughty boys and girls with toys. From now on his gifts were doled out solely for children who were well-behaved throughout the year. Rich and poor kids alike could attain the same level of Christmas minus the fortune. Mr Claus assumed he'd figured out a way to save Xmas forever. Unfortunately, forever wasn't as long he thought.

# CHAPTER 3

## The Challenge

Father Christmas altered his operation entirely and was on the verge of relocating. He knew he couldn't stay in a populated area as the attention and exposure grew. Kids waited outside his home on a daily basis, sometimes even missing school. On holidays like Easter and half-term they lingered behind his workshop to see if he'd discard any toys he deemed unworthy. In the space of two Christmases Mr Claus became the most famous person in the world. Now word had been passed around he got pelted with more Xmas lists than years gone by. Each December his workload doubled, then tripled and then quadrupled. Every night he came home ate his supper, drank alcohol and crashed on their couch. Father Christmas by all accounts was an unhealthy fellow.

'Honey, this whole thing's getting way out of control. I've got children snooping in my dustbins and adults attempting to break into my workshop,' he said, highly frustrated.

'You asked for it.' Mrs Claus could be a harsh woman and she had to be Mr Claus's thoughtfulness would see him give the shirt off his back.

'I get no time to myself anymore. I'm always on the go,' he complained.

'What did you think would happen? Christmas happens every year, you know.'

'I'm thinking this year shall be my last; we'll go back to the old ways.'

Mrs Claus left the dishes in the sink to soak. 'You're living in a dreamland. Imagine what the public would do once they heard the great toy maker Nicholas Claus is no more.' Father Christmas had a vivid imagination; he foresaw a world where kids cried and whined, ending up miserable year by year with empty stockings. 'Alright you made your point. However, I won't continue in this vein.'

When morning broke over another dull, dreary December day, Father Christmas posted several vacancies on a notice-board in the town centre. It read.

HELP WANTED. EMPLOYER REQUIRES FULL TIME WORKERS EAGER TO MANUFACTURE TOYS. ALL APPLICANTS MUST BE HARDWORKING, PUNC-TUAL, POLITE, CARING AND CONSIDERATE. NO PRIOR EXPERIENCE NEEDED. ACCOMODATION WILL BE PROVIDED. ANY APPLICANTS APPROVED SHOULD BE READY TO WORK RIGHT AWAY.

Many people applied and lots weren't suitable. Mr Claus was a really picky person; no one seemed good enough to work in such a wonderful establishment. For a while Father Christmas felt he'd be burdened with bringing the nation's Christmas alone. Then he received a few visitors in the form of six unemployed elves. They'd recently been laid off from sweeping chimneys as families found their children small enough to do the same duty. As you may fathom, job options for an elf are pretty limited and jobs that paid well were virtually unheard of. Once they read Father Christmas' ad, they knew it'd be ideal. All six elves dressed in their Sunday best and all wrote out impressive resumes.

'We heard through the grapevine you're looking for some valuable employees. Well we answered your call,' said one of the elves in his squeaky manner.

Father Christmas viewed their references and was ultimately blown away by how much they offered to his company.

'You do realise we're moving to a land far away?' Mr Claus explained.

'That's fine; we love to travel. We can adapt to any circumstances,' said the elf. They'd already packed their suitcases.

'You're hired. We're leaving this weekend.'

Mr Claus picked a spot somewhere blissfully serene although very, very cold.

His wife wasn't too happy about the sudden shift to a cooler climate, although she recognised Mr Claus needed peace and quiet to be productive. And let me tell you there's no place on Earth more tranquil than the North Pole. The couple first travelled to frozen land in 1822; its terrific snowy white scenery and vacant land felt perfect for Father Christmas.

He built a massive estate for him and his elves.

As of today, Mr Claus' business is an all-year gig. Before, he used to get at least a couple months downtime, but as soon as one Christmas was over, he began working on the next one. Every February for numerous generations Father Christmas was presented with a fitness test to show he was still capable of pulling off what his career demanded. You must appreciate the intensity of Xmas. Decade after decade can wear down the strongest of men. Father Christmas displayed significant aging; his bones cracked and clicked and the thick grey head of hair dramatically thinned. He walked around in a slow, ponderous way. Doctors told him he needed a knee replacement and probably at best could continue as Father Claus for maybe a year or two tops; that was nine long years ago. Mr Claus donned his famed red suit, preparing for the physical assignment in his bedroom. He stared in the mirror observing the extra timber he carried; his belt buckled on the last punch hole.

'I don't think I'm up to spec this time' love.'

'You say that every single year and pull one out the bag,' said Mrs Claus.

To be fair, Father Claus only qualified last time round by the narrowest margin, one thousandth of a second.

'Something is different. I smell it in the air, I can taste it on my tongue.'

'Oh, give over, stop being such a drama queen.'

'You don't get it. All my life I've been the Christmas guy. That's what my days have consisted of,' groaned an upset Mr Claus.

'Someday you knew it was gonna end. You weren't the first Father Claus, but if a poll was taken, you'd be ranked the best with a bullet,' comforted Mrs Claus hugging him.

A daunting knock rattled their bedroom door disturbing them both.

'Ready or not dad, we're waiting,' I said.

Mr Claus had three children: Nicholas Claus V (me) and my brother and sister who we'll meet later. As for me, being the firstborn, I still lived at home at age thirty-eight. To you it seems bizarre, but traditionally all Father Christmas' eldest sons never leave the nest. His father before him stayed and so and so forth.

At nine o'clock sharpish a variety of obstacles were laid out on the North Pole's sprawling land.

An elf brought out a stopwatch to time proceedings. Mr Claus stretched his withering limbs and joints. The challenge presented Father Christmas with a series of physical tasks. First, he'd have to sprint over to his sleigh and shove no less than thirty gifts into his sack before dragging it to the top of the hill.

Once there, Father Claus should round up his eight reindeer, secure them and then reach the finish line inside seven minutes.

'You got the keys to victory, sir.'

'We've got ultimate faith in you, sir,' hailed the Elves who adored him. There is no telling where they'd be if his grandfather didn't employ their family members.

A very pensive Mr Claus arrived at the start line; he waved at the encouraging crowd rather gingerly. In all my years watching him perform he'd never looked so intimidated. Heavy snow fell on the track; this weather allowed Father Christmas to change his footwear. As soon as he settled on the right choice of shoe the challenge begun. A loud gun signalled the timer to start. An enormous scream propelled Father Claus to forget his nagging body. He rallied over to his sack still slipping and sliding in the thick snow.

'Go! Go! Go! Go!' cheered the Elves.

Mr Claus slammed every present into the sack, drawing the string shut. Then it became visibly clear his strength wasn't there anymore. Usually Father Christmas hoisted the sack over one shoulder and hurried towards his sleigh. However, today he tussled with the full sack, struggling to lift it. This hampered his time incredibly. He was gassing increasingly, breathing harder. Step by step he slowed heading for his sleigh.

'Come on dad, push through it,' I shouted.

'Thought you'd be the one rooting against him, to get your turn in the hot seat,' replied Mrs Claus a.k.a (mom).

I contemplated the consequences if Father Christmas couldn't pass the challenge. I prayed and pleaded he'd somehow turn this one around. Unfortunately, Mr Claus looked out on his feet. Five minutes of time was gobbled away, and the sleigh wasn't even halfway up the hill. The Elves were very apprehensive as to whether he still stood a legitimate chance. Soon attention shifted to me; Elves began pointing and chatting intently.

'Stay focused! Drive, father!' I yelled.

As determined as a caged animal, Father Claus summoned up all his might and surged carving a path through the powdery snow. His muscles flexed as he grunted along, finally approaching the hilltop. Still lagging in the time department, his fierce will had reignited my hopes.

One minute fifty remained. All that was left was for him to shackle his reindeer and speed to the finish line. In my opinion reindeer are probably the most intelligent animals ever. One high-pitched whistle and a bunch of charging antlers flew into view. Father Claus harnessed each reindeer securely then bolted to a thunderous ovation. The elves weren't too keen on me. There's something about the boss' son in every workplace which employees dislike. Anyway, provided Mr Claus completed the obstacle course, I'd receive another year without feeling their full hatred. His reindeer were doing their darnedest, dumping mountains of snow aside. Father Claus masterfully steered the sleigh downhill.

'Thirty seconds left,' hollered mother.

Elves stared at their different stopwatches in desperation. No one wanted a changing of the guard, me included. Sadly, the heavens strongly believed otherwise and did everything in their power to decide matters. Bundles of snow pelted down at a blizzard-like rate, temporarily killing the reindeer's sight. Father Christmas eased up, allowing them to adjust. Their relentlessly acceleration halted meaning time played a huge factor once more. Elves worked tirelessly to clear the finish line; flickering orange lights were erected to draw the reindeer's attention. All their efforts were squandered as the reindeer battled against elements greater than themselves and gradually laboured home in a dismal seven minutes forty-two. Disappointment riddled the North Pole. Elves sobbed, consoling one another. Some had only served under one Father Christmas so knew no other way. Tragically, Mr Claus had failed and the day we all dreaded was dawning.

# CHAPTER 4

## The Ceremony

So, for the third time Father Christmas' legendary role would change hands. Whenever a new Father Claus was to be crowned a formal ceremony had to take place within one week. For me to officially be considered Father Claus there was a lot red tape to go through. I had a vision test, blood tests, strength assessment and psychological exams. Yeah, some of you may perceive this is all a tad too extreme. However, the stress and commitment have a serious effect. It put my great-grandfather into an early grave and forced my grandfather to retire prematurely. Needless to say, by the time the night was out I'd leaped through numerous hoops. I successfully cleared all evaluations and tomorrow would be unveiled to the elves as St Nicholas IV.

As tomorrow came a strange atmosphere grabbed hold of the North Pole. An unusual mildness prevailed, and small rays of sunshine peeked over the mountains. The day seemed so casual even polar bears and penguins visiting from the south, hung out with each other. Have you ever woken up in the same bed, in the same house, in the same surroundings, yet everything is entirely different? Well, this just happened to me. The weight of responsibility rested heavy on my back. All this expectation and all I wanted to do was roll over and sleep. 4 A.M now became my daily start time. I knew certain people got up before the sun, but I didn't know I'd be one of them. Yesterday I was just the son of a man who ran Christmas for boys and girls all across the globe. Today I run a workforce of loyal elves ready to deliver another epic Xmas. There's two ways to go with pressure; you'll either rise to it or disintegrate under the burden. That morning I wondered to myself, could my stage be any bigger? When you compare me to previous Father Clauses their transitions were much easier. The original handover occurred in 1885; then roughly between one hundred to three hundred million children received gifts. When my father was ushered in on February 6th, 1948 close to a billion kids existed. In our ever-expanding population there are currently nearly two billion of you little rascals. That's a significant jump, especially for your debut. It's hard to get my head around producing that many presents annually.

'Wake up, half the day's over,' said mother.

As I lumbered from my cosy lair a whole heap of upheaval transpired. Mom and father were gathering all their items out the master bedroom, numerous elves assisting them.

'What's going on?' I asked, caught unaware.

Mother tenderly kissed my cheek. 'The master room goes to the master of the house. Congratulation, son. Words cannot express my happiness and pride.'

'Good day to be you,' snarled an Elf.

'Lucky, lucky boy,' added another disgruntled Elf carrying boxes.

Shame I didn't feel so lucky. My worst nightmare is now my doomed reality.

'Where will you go?'

'For the time being we'll remain in the guest room until we decide on a destination,' exclaimed mom; she'd already earmarked the Bahamas as a suitable retirement location.

'I can't picture myself here alone,' I moaned. Initially we were a fivesome: mom, dad, me, my younger sister Jackie and brother Terrell. Plus, how can if forget the dozen or so elves who were like extended family. However, without father and his gentle giant personality charming the elves, I doubt I'll be so warmly received once he's gone.

'You'll be fine; we're not leaving tomorrow. I'll be here to ease your transition,' said the ex-Father Christmas in a sorrowful way. I gauged he wasn't mentally ready to let go of the sleigh and reindeer.

That afternoon the ceremony was set, and a banqueting feast was made up of the freshest food.

Outside caterers created some of the most scrumptious dishes: deep-fried crab claws, chicken casserole, succulent lamb shanks, soft fluffy mashed potatoes and crunchy vegetables. For dessert, a Christmas themed cake built to resemble the North Pole. Mother brought out her finest cutlery and covered the table in a festive cloth.

I couldn't shake how fancy the occasion was. A pianist played delightful music throughout the lengthy proceedings. Father seemed very morbid; his face drooped as if someone had attached a kettle bell to his chin. His famous upbeat outlook soured. It's a shocking moment when you realise you'll never be that magical guy again. In front of his former adoring staff, he grinned and told funny stories. The elves dressed in matching three-piece suits were all clean-shaven and appeared rather dashing. As for father he relinquished his glorious seat at the head of the table.

'That's not my rightful place anymore,' he grumbled, taking up a position further down. 'The head of the house-hold deserves the head seat. Treat her right and she'll serve you well.'

He begrudgingly shook my hand, pushing down with enough force to crush every knuckle. I think it's a dad thing; as they get older their superiority dissolves. First you grow taller, get stronger, become smarter and then they begin to rely on you. To him the dreaded role-reversal was transpiring. All my guests stood patiently waiting for me to take the chair.

'Come on, be seated, we're getting cramp,' said mother.

At the head of the table I thought an overwhelming trans-formation of power and influence would takeover. All of a sudden, I'd comprehend what and how to do anything Father Christmases before me did. And yet nothing. The wooden chair rocked awkwardly; father's portly body had destroyed its legs and it squeaked with any slight movement. A mellow mood filtered into the room; no one wanted to speak. The monumental handover was turning into a damp squib.

Mother, who had probably enjoyed a couple of sherries too many by this point, clinked her glass. 'Let me be the one to congratulate this man, my firstborn, on his promotion. I'm sure my husband has few wonderful words of support.'

Father glared at mother, highly annoyed. He'd have preferred to remain silent. She persisted, nudging and budging him until he surrendered.

The Elves all listened respectfully.

'OK, I'd like to personally show gratitude to my previous employees who diligently worked their tail ends off decade after decade. Truly, from the core of my heart, thank you. The honour is all mine.'

'The pleasure was ours and nobody will ever replace you,' sobbed Elf Fletcher.

A few Elves fought back the tears. Those that couldn't politely excused themselves.

'Now regrettably there comes a time where everything great, beautiful and magnificent will cease. Sooner or later we'll all be worm food.' Father wasn't exactly lightening the tone. 'However, today is a day that promises hope. A new era in how we prepare for Christmas. A new face has arrived at the helm. I'm sure you'll do your utmost to make his transformation as comfortable and painless as possible. There is no person I'd rather see supplant me than my very own flesh and blood.'

'I can think of several better choices,' mumbled an unsatisfied Elf.

'He'll make his share of errors and mistakes. Every rookie should be allowed a settling-in phase. So, without any delays let's collectively welcome my lad into the superb life of Father Christmas.'

A meteoric ovation echoed from a dozen tiny hands, sounding like a thousand firecrackers. They expected me to make an inspiring speech, something that'd prove I'd be able to fill those prestigious black boots. But how could I even suggest I was worthy of replacing the greatest Father Christmas ever? Nearly every year I watched my old man scrape by, barely filling his obligations. Some scenarios it is better to be authentic and speak from the heart. In others, you lie your behind off.

As a ritual, dad placed down his iconic red and white bobble hat which signalled a new Father Claus has been declared.

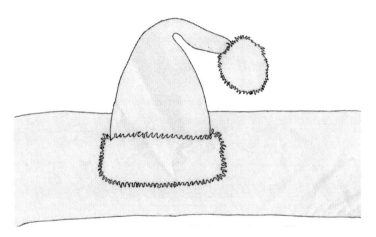

I confidently gazed around the room, giving out an impression of utter control. I quickly demanded the pianist halted his fantastic music with a brutal throat slashing gesture. The guests gasped in complete surprise at how I handled things. They interpreted me as a ruthless leader who had zero tolerance.

The nervous pianist abruptly stopped mid song.

'Thank you all for coming out. Now listen up,' I stammered. My upper body appeared broad and strong, but beneath the table though my legs frantically shook. 'Most children want to emulate their fathers and I'm no different. Routinely I fantasised about one day being the man you all cherish. Make no mistake about it, my work ethic can and will rival that of any Father Christmas in history.'

A couple of Elves bought my ridiculous speech. Obviously, the majority saw it for what it was, a smoke screen.

'Work ethic? You've never worked a day in your life lad,' a very well-respected Elf sniped.

I could've taken the high road and ignored his insult, but I saw this as a chance to make a statement. I marched over to the mouthy elf. 'Would you like to repeat that comment for the rest of us?'

The brash elf didn't cower away, as I'd predicted. Instead he boldly recited his words with extras. 'Face facts, you're a winner by default. You've earned nought. Just another undeserving spoilt boy piggybacking off daddy's success.'

I'm certain a lot of the elves had a similar feeling. My authority was definitely being challenged and tested. I didn't have much to worry about because, when you're the boss, you do the hiring and the firing. 'I want you to recognise what's not acceptable. If you befriend me, you'll find me nothing more than reasonable, although I do have a mean side too.'

The Elf pretended to quiver in fear. 'Oh, he's so intimidating,' he blabbed.

My eyes filled with rage; a scorching fury ravished my brain. 'Take your narrow-mindedness and see the door, you Debbie downer,' I barked.

'Pardon me,' he said, shaking.

'Take that dumbfounded expression and seek employment elsewhere.' I quickly established a new regime using a powerful strategy of heartlessness. Love it or loathe it, the elves would learn their place.

# CHAPTER 5

## Finding my Feet

Becoming the boss of any company can bring a lot of strain, stress and ultimately unrest. Since I'd fired one of if not the most respected elf, my approval rating had plummeted. Animosity between me and the other elves remained unresolved. Anything asked of them was met with sarcastic remarks, evil looks or sometimes not done at all. I'd go on record to say this year was shaping up to be the worst Christmas full stop and it was only mid-February. Thankfully, father kept a level of professionalism and around the ranks they still held him on a pedestal. He pulled us all together from time to time. Overall, our relationship was estranged and that's putting it mildly. Weeks went by in the workshop where silence lingered. Elves worked their shifts and left without as much as a hello or goodbye.

I wish being a hated boss was my sole problem; that I could handle to an extent, but Father Christmas has many duties, none more so than flying. See here's another urban legend—people think it's true that we use reindeer to fly.

Now anyone with two brain cells, eyes, logic or any sort of common sense understands the only living entities which can fly are birds and insects. Yes, you heard me, reindeer CAN'T FLY. They can do plenty of brilliant activities, but flying is not one of them. So what I am saying? Stick with me. I don't want to dispel the notion that Santa whisks through the air with his exceptional reindeer because that part is correct. As my grandfather's Christmas role gained more exposure no longer could he deliver goods on foot. He appeared stumped; the thought of scurrying about like a headless chicken for another year wouldn't be efficient, especially as his gift giving service kept increasing. On a shivering cold winter night at the North Pole, but when is it not freezing? No, seriously, you guys. I've officially glimpsed the sun twice. Anyway, in a bold move, Father Christmas II, who many consider the smartest version, gathered he'd be capable of reaching more homes through the air than on his feet. Now, internal combustion engines were in their infancy. They were very hard to come by and quite pricey in those days. My grandfather was a clever old geezer. His ability to construct any object by simply scanning a blueprint or manual is revered amongst my family. He purchased spare aircraft engine parts where possible, and after finishing his daily jobs went to work on motorising his sleigh. Obviously, nobody succeeds on their first attempt and nor did he. Following several crashes, two blown engines and numerous injuries (including a broken tailbone which prevented him from sitting down for eight months) he finally came out victorious.

On December 6th 1921 Father Christmas cleared the ground on a dry run. The positives were overwhelming, mainly due to reducing his time. Nonetheless, happiness didn't last. As soon as he loaded his sack and harnessed his horses ground clearance disappeared.

'She's too heavy up front,' he griped.

The following day Father Christmas ditched the horses; their bulky frames were no good for an aerial performance. With the steeds gone, he knew some creature had to replace them. Originally, he tried a pack of wolves; the result was frightening, and they literally tore chunks out of each other.

'They're too aggressive! You can't treat them like pets,' he screamed.

Father Claus scrapped the wolf pack, opting for a group of husky dogs; they were similar in size and willing to be coached. He assumed he'd fixed his issues until it came to stopping. The dogs weren't strong enough, their paws sliding in the thick snow. Whilst the huskies showed promise, safety was too much of a factor.

Frustration intensified and his head throbbed every night. Many times in life things happen by sheer coincidence. On a mid-afternoon stroll on his North Pole residence, a lost animal staggered into Father Christmas' path.

The confused animal looked exhausted; his antlers were chipped and cracked. He did own the brightest red nose ever seen though. It usually led to ridicule from various animals. However, the compassion my grandfather displayed by feeding him calmed the reindeer from any antics.

He analysed the animal's unique dimensions and deemed its solid body was powerful enough to propel his sleigh, the hooves were ideal for braking and its weight was perfect for flight and stability.

'You shall be Rudolph,' he gleamed.

Absolutely no adjustments were required. He hitched Dasher, Prancer, Vixen, Comet, Cupid, Donner, Blitzen and Rudolph, gliding through the air like so.

There's another history lesson for you. I gradually began my transition into Christmas' leading man. I had final say on everything. Overseeing my new sleigh, I broke away from the tradition by selecting a glistening gold and white colour scheme with my picture graced across the side. My chair inside the sleigh was completely comprised of the spongiest foam and smoothest cowhide. I also upgraded the outdated A-Z maps father used for a hip Sat Nav. Some bitter elves felt I'd lost the concept of Santa Claus and made it more about me than the children. Of all days, today came my biggest baptism of fire an unassisted flying exam. And I was bricking myself.

Father laid out a runway and landing strip then gave me some wise advice.

'Bring it in, son,' he called. 'This is the trickiest part of your evolution; conquer the flying and the rest will fall into place. These reindeer are intelligent, they follow strict commands. Don't be overly violent on the reins; a slight tug left or right and they'll quickly change direction. One yank and they go, two sharp tugs to stop, the rest comes with instinct. The engine is controlled by your feet exactly like an automatic car brake and accelerator.'

I got myself comfortable in the driver's seat, wrapping both reindeer leashes around my fist.

'Take it steady; the speed can be surprising,' he informed.

Adrenaline fizzled inside me. I was going to fly solo. Father started the aircraft engine, its propeller forcing the clogging snow to disperse.

'Remember, let the reindeer reach the cliff before accelerating.'

Upon hearing the motor chattering behind, the animals gathered it was go time. They all simultaneously leaped into motion. Their synchronised rhythm was something to behold. My metal sled glided along patted down snow. Take-off in a Christmas sleigh has a fair few key-components that need fine balancing. There is speed; one mile too fast or slow can be the difference between triumph and tragedy. Timing: if I'm too eager I'll cause a power overload, resulting in a massive explosion. And lastly accuracy; there two red markers I must navigate through to find the altitude to maintain a sustainable flying height. Mother worried over my flying debut, like mothers do. She demanded they fitted airbags, racing seatbelts which restricted mobility, protective goggles and an anti-roll bar. To be honest, how my father, grandfather and great-grandfather before him avoided permanent damage or death is a total miracle. I'm glad she overruled father and made all these safety precautions mandatory. As the reindeer pounded, pummelled and thrashed we edged near take-off. I noticed some rebellious elves hung a poster outside their window labelling me a "Mommy's Lil Baby

Boy." I was livid and gestured towards the rotten faced, tiny people who were having laughing fits.

'I'll run you terrible swine into the ground, you watch me,' I fumed. In reality I should've concentrated on what's necessary, perfecting the art of flight. They bugged the heck out of me and I got riled up to the brink of erupting. In anger I squeezed the reindeer harnesses tightly. The animals took this as a signal and decelerated.

Father, a master at flying, pinpointed my lack of momentum and hysterically hollered, yelled and screamed. 'Brake! Brake son!'

His concern brought mother outside in just a t-shirt, skirt and socks. The sub-zero conditions had no effect on her. What's weather when you're observing your child's demise? 'Don't stand there, do something!' she panicked.

Father froze; he shrugged, knowing my fortunes lay with God. 'He's helpless love,' dad croaked, bending to one knee and making the sign of cross along his chest.

The reindeer plodded on minus the thrust and energy. I approached the cliff, essentially dawdling, when I thumped the gas pedal.

The elves peeked out their windows hearing mother's ghastly shrieks. Though animosity persisted behind closed doors, my death would be a horrific affair. The engine rattled. Its piston furiously rotated up and down; they were attempting to regain the impetus lost by the reindeer. I'd completely mentally shut down and begun entertaining thoughts of the afterlife. Was there actually a heaven? And am I on the list? Spinning propeller blades ramped up to their maximum speed. The reindeer leapt up; having no more snow to pound upon they tucked in their legs. My thumping heart ceased to beat. I watched the animals nervously awaiting their bodies to nosedive. Father always told me to prevent a crash focus on where you want to go rather than where you're likely to head. I visualised myself gliding above the pale hills and momentarily, we were air bound marginally escaping the instant smash.

'Hurrah! That's my boy. Way to go,' applauded Dad.

Mother relaxed her facial frowns and wrinkles smoothed out. 'My prayers have been answered.' I managed to achieve a favourable flying height and the reindeer blissfully went along for the ride. Feeling a little cocky I tried some flying techniques only a seasoned professional should try. I cranked on the accelerator, cutting through the sky in a figure of eight. I kept soaring, hitting the throttle again, this time going upside down and completing an impressive loop.

'What are you doing man?' vented dad, kicking his feet in the snow.

'I'm living it large.' I smiled and arrogantly nodded, sizing up my next exercise, an extremely difficult rolling scissors. To succeed in a trick with such a degree of skill man and animal must have the ultimate trust built up over years of bonding. I didn't allow for this to transpire so when I zigged the irritated reindeer zagged, throwing us off balance. In haste I ragged their harnesses harshly, annoying them further. They howled then acted out by sticking their legs out creating excessive down force.

'You idiot, come off the gas,' yelled dad blowing his gasket.

The disobedient reindeer were now doing the opposite of whatever I intended. Father left out the part about what to do when your reindeer decide to go rogue.

'Don't brake! You need to level out before landing,' he nervously instructed.

'How? For pity's sake how?' I went into full panic mode, jamming on the brakes, which sent the reindeer nuts. Their antlers erratically twitched as they figured things weren't going well. We began to descend rapidly quite some distance from our designated landing strip. Although the engine wasn't running, the gliding speed still carried a punch. Due to fact the reindeer wouldn't let me steer we viciously slammed into ground. Their hooves deployed the emergency stop procedure, stabbing the snow. The space needed wasn't there and it resulted with us crashing straight into the workshop entrance.

*Wallop!*

# CHAPTER 6

## The First Outing

I sustained some deep cuts and bruises, a cracked rib and a hairline fracture in my right foot, but most of all the one thing I hurt was my ego. Apart from a few war wounds which healed in ample time I gauged my first flight a hit. Although several reindeer didn't fare as favourably, especially Randolph (grandson of the illustrious Rudolph). Rudolph in his off season was a busy old boy, becoming rather popular with the lady reindeer. Not to go into lewd detail let's just say the red-nosed lady's man fathered countless kids who took on the family trade. Nobody ever possessed Rudolph's abilities, but Randolph had his moments. The injuries Randolph suffered cost him a promising career. The remaining reindeer were patched up and persevered, although all faith in me was lost. My sleigh was a written off too, the mangled engine exploded catching fire. Thankfully, I purchased an insurance package that covered me under any circumstance. Within one week of filing a claim my brand spanking new replacement sleigh arrived, bigger, faster, brasher and indestructible. After all, it is illegal to operate a vehicle without valid insurance.

Father seethed. His disgust at my bravado lasted months. In an effort to deflect the blame I pointed to an engine fault causing me to act irrationally. After a full investigation provided zero evidence dad understood I was full of it. His disappointment kept on growing until it finally reached a head on a memorable Thursday morning. This Thursday in particular my workshop entrance was being rebuilt and again I had some new modifications. In the original blueprint everything was expected to return to its boring self. The plain wood grain work counters, ordinary dull lighting, grey carpet and unfashionable wallpaper. I viewed Father Claus desperately needed an upgrade, so I selected glossy wooden floors and bought all the elves roller skates to roll from station to station. The walls were painted in a shimmering gold. I also threw out the enormous factory style light bulbs for elegant wall fitted lights which shone either side of each workstation instead of just above. For entertainment speakers were mounted at every station pumping out jolly Christmas tunes.

I made a work environment you'd rejoice in. The elves found it difficult to find flaws with my new layout. They won't acknowledge it, but their perky smiles and occasional exchanging of words meant they'd mellowed. Whilst the contractors remodelled, mother and father enjoyed their first holiday in forty plus years. Upon his return on Thursday, father saw the very last spirit of Father Christmas evaporate. I thought he'd be pleased I'd used my initiative. Well, I thought wrong.

'You're impressed, aren't you?' I asked.

He slammed his coat down disturbed by the changing surroundings. 'What have you done?'

'We tried to tell him.'

'Some people are just too stubborn,' claimed two elves, basically selling me out.

I had always been slightly intimidated by father's bold voice, bulky frame and gruff beard. However, something came over me that day. 'It has better lighting, easier access and more space. Just because you're blind to it doesn't me it isn't beneficial, right guys?'

The elves collectively lost their voices, unwilling to engaging in eye contact.

'You're a moron, boy. You don't get it. Do you think it's some game? First the outrageous sleigh, now the workshop. What's next, delivering the presents on boxing day?' he raged.

'Oh, get over yourself. I spruced up an old shabby concept. In my books a long overdue remodelling took place. You should thank me,' I bitterly replied.

'We've got traditional values you destroyed in order of being self-centred.' He gradually stepped forward, imposing his surreal size advantage.

Today though, I wasn't backing down either. We literally butted head I could smell the pickled onions he ate for lunch.

'So, you're Johnny big time now.' He aggressively shoved me in the chest.

'All I'm saying maybe this Father Claus lark ain't so gruelling if things are done right,' I sniped.

Father grunted, His nostrils swelled, his teeth grated against one another as every inch of his body fought the urge to take a swing at me. The worst insult to any Father Christmas is to downplay their credentials. 'We are through. You've made your choice and obviously heritage and honour mean little to nothing. Don't think of coming to me for any friendly advice.'

'Finally, you say something I can agree with,' I grinned.

True to his word, father left me to my own devices. He felt I pushed him out before his time. I didn't set out to hurt his feelings, but to make an omelette you can't be afraid to crack a few eggs. Father and son dynamics are complicated; you're never sure where you stand. This near violent confrontation had us in a place we both weren't comfortable with. Neither of us knew how to respond to the other. The friction lasted quite a while and the North Pole suffered immeasurably.

We reached December 1st and there was no sign of reconciling. Regardless of the problems at home, my schedule was crammed between Christmas pre-orders I had to make and my official debut as Santa Claus in Lapland. Most Father Christmases looked forward to this public outing; it was considered the Holy Grail. In some ways it's a home from home the Arctic weather, ice-covered lakes and the powdery coating of snow. Lapland and the North Pole must be distant cousins or something. Nonetheless, my duty wasn't to admire the stunning beauty, ski nor visit any of Finland's great tourist attractions. My single agenda is to meet and greet the young boys and girls in the world's oldest and largest grotto ever constructed. The building lay unoccupied for a majority of the year; children knew about it yet didn't dare go inside without adult consent. The grotto took several months to finish and was hidden away far beyond the cities, town, slopes and hills or any ski resort. The remote area is only accessible by boat and takes four hours travelling wise. I'm glad this is a one-off. My grandfather made this trip mandatory for all new Father Clauses. I still appreciate certain historical customs.

A guide carefully rowed us across the crumbling lake as the ice melted beneath us. He was jolly bloke in his colourful jumper and Wellington boots. 'You're the new kid around town?'

'Guilty as charged I'm Father Claus IV,' I answered.

He beamed, getting rather giddy. 'I can't believe the actual Santa is in my presence.'

His overreaction startled me. I never thought about how my promotion affected my world status.

The guide began fiddling in his pockets grabbing his phone. 'Santa, please can I take a selfie?'

'Sure, anything for a fan,' I said.

He attached his mobile to a selfie stick and mushed his face next to mine. 'Say Christmas.'

The phone's bright flash almost blinded us. 'This is going straight on my wall.' He

posted: Me chillin with Santa! #RealFatherClaus #Lapland #reindeer.

His message went out to every one of his 769 followers who reposted it to their followers. Soon Finland's five million residents knew Santa was in the house.

Their responses were overwhelmingly positive; children forced their parents to hire boats. Such was the obsession some even contemplated swimming to the island. Every child dreams of meeting the real Santa not the phony ones employed by supermarkets and parties.

We stepped off the boat and before I entered the magnificent grotto elated screams erupted. I could see the grotto's wooden panels shudder and vibrate as kids packed in the building. Behind me hundreds of boats carrying jubilant children and disgruntled adults were sailing along the lake. If I ever wondered about the power of the social networks, now I knew.

I strutted up and down outside, too nervous to enter. My training hadn't taught me the subtle nature of Father Claus. Santa has a magical way with children; he can silence them in seconds. Wild chants reverberated from inside the grotto.

'Santa! Santa! Santa!'

I felt a shell of myself. The usually warm and cuddly red Santa suit now restricted me. I loosened the belt buckle trying to grab some extra breaths.

My guide watched on profoundly. In his mind, Father Claus doesn't lack confidence. 'What's up man? The admiration of many kids beckons.'

'I'm not ready. I'm not ready. These kids will see my inexperience and I won't recover. They'll hate me.'

The guide chuckled. 'Hate? In their eyes your support is paramount. Provided you don't kill anybody whatever you say and do will suffice.'

With his comments ringing in my ears I composed my juddering body and strolled into the massive grotto. Fake snow dropped from the ceiling as trumpets churned out Christmas songs. Excited kids were totally speechless. Their tiny heads followed me step by step. The fabulous arena played into every Father Christmas misconception; a dummy Santa hung upside down in a chimney whilst reindeer sat on the roof.

'Ho, ho, ho, merry Christmas folks,' I announced, gaining in self-belief.

The guide's theory couldn't have been more spot on. I owned the room. Half a dozen helpers waved me to my personal space, where a throne was awaiting me next to a beautiful log filled fireplace. A long stream of kids ranging from short, fat, tall, slim toddlers to early teens and everything in between patiently stood behind a rope. The whole grotto thing is pretty easy to figure out. One child at a time sits on my lap, tells me what they want for Christmas and so long as they behave well, I'll grant their wish. This worked fine initially but try sitting on an uncomfortable chair with snotty kids spitting in your earhole. My backside had fallen asleep and due to the weight of a handful of kids both thighs were starting to burn. The endless number of children continued, more arrived on boats and barges throughout the night. Hungry, weary, angry and desperate for a toilet break I maintained a false level of enthusiasm until Jeremy. Jeremy is one of those children your parents warn you about. He had chubby hands that remained sticky no matter how much he washed them and wore clothes two sizes smaller. I saw him picking boogers and wiping them on his t-shirt beforehand. The disgusting kid sauntered over a strange scent of vinegar followed him.

'Greetings, young child,' I said, grimacing.

He aggressively hopped on my lap, jarring my knee; I faintly squealed.

'I want a voice activated drone, not a pesky remote control one,' he demanded.

'I'll see what I can do.'

'Don't see, promise me,' Jeremy said, getting hyperactive.

'Santa never makes promises, especially when it depends on your manners,' I explained.

He bobbed out his gross tongue, flicking spit drenching my jacket. 'Promise! Promise! Promise!'

'Calm down, you brat,' I raised my voice a hint.

'You promise me! You promise me!' Jeremy hissed, becoming overexcited.

'Listen, you'll wind up with a lump of coal.'

Jeremy's body language altered, his movement stopping entirely.

'Oh no, not again.'

I had no idea what he meant until I felt a damp spot appearing on my trousers. Ultimately the little lad, overcome with emotions, had burst his bladder, relieving himself directly onto my leg. Wetting yourself is one embarrassment but someone peeing on you is inexcusable.

I angrily hauled Jeremy into the main room, publicly shaming him. 'You despicable cockroach. You horrible creature. You flea-filled dirtbag. You terrible termite.'

Jeremy quivered and crumbled. Tears consumed his light green eyes as he blubbered, running to his parents. The mood shifted to one of hostility. The crowd threw cups, chairs, used abusive language and offensive gestures to be disrespectful.

I responded, giving them what for. 'You stupid people don't deserve Christmas.'

As far as first public showings go, let's not sugar coat it, this was a monumental disaster.

# CHAPTER 7

## Brotherly & Sisterly Love

Crazy Santa was the most searched video on the internet. A wave of trolls commented on how appallingly I had acted. I gained national press; newspaper articles were written and to boost sales they elaborated the story. In one piece I was a savage evil lunatic who preyed on little kids. Some said I had a brutal previous past as a vicious bareknuckle fighter. All these allegations were fabricated. Various new companies and mainstream media channels swamped my North Pole home offering feature length interviews. Mother notified me that coming home wasn't a good plan. Cable outlets were hounding my parents daily, causing them much distress and inconvenience. They should expect my legal representative to make contact.

For now, I took a short break. My head was a swirl of poison. I sort of went into hiding. It was necessary to lie low until the heat died down. I left my most trusted elves in charge; what could go wrong there? A whole hell of a lot. The only places I knew I could stay undetected was a place where I'd feel the love and not have my character analysed. If you remember me saying I had two younger siblings Terrell and Jackie. As kids we were close. I protected them like older brothers should. At school, no kids messed around with Terrell or Jackie because they'd have me to face. As we grow up, people seemingly drift apart. They'll have their interests; you'll have yours and then you'll meet up sparingly. However, there's something ingrained in all humans, which means when you've hit rock bottom your family will automatically rally behind you.

My sister married the love of her life and quickly laid down roots in the sunshine state that is Florida. Considering Jackie was the baby, she appeared wise beyond her years. Her high intelligence made communicating so difficult. Have you ever been around somebody who instantly make you feel thick? Well, Jackie usually had you searching a dictionary for definitions of words. Jackie was a funny old sort; her hair was always kept in a bun like a librarian. The clothes she wore looked plucked straight out of Victorian times. She owned a vast collection of baggy skirts that touched her ankles and Victorian hats which covered her face. She passed this weird dress sense to her three daughters. They lived in a modest home in Orlando. Once you've spent two plus decades in the frozen setting of the North Pole you simply run to the sun. Their beautiful home actually opened out onto the soft crumbly sand. Jackie, well aware of my predicament, treated me fantastically. She offered up a room with a sensational balcony view; the gushing blue ocean brought along a delightful calmness. It gave me time to think. I leaned on the railings, speculating how to turn this sinking ship around.

Jackie hadn't seen me since I stepped up as Father Claus. She constantly congratulated me.

'My big bro Santa! I'm gobsmacked.'
'Hurrah for me! Life's now one big picnic.'

She sharply jabbed me with her elbow. 'You are Mr Grumpy. Hasn't anyone told you life is solely up to you? So the Lapland was a calamitous, dreadful, horrid, outrageous, pitiful, downright catastrophe.'

'Alright, I get it. Weren't you supposed to be cheering me up?' I interrupted.

'They hate you now, but there's a silver lining staring you point blank in the face,' said Jackie.

'And that would be?'

'You've suffered the worst possible start and you're still living and breathing. Things can only get better. If anybody is capable of turning a negative into a positive, it's you.'

'I'm at a loss. Have you ever thought some people aren't meant for certain jobs, like president, racing driver, or Santa Claus?' I said frustratedly

'Nah, not you. Claus men are built of sterner stuff. Christmas is your vocation, no doubt about it. I guarantee in the future we'll laugh over this as the tipping point to brighter days.'

See, that's what I missed: a pleasant influence. For her olden girl style Jackie's wit and wisdom came as a brilliant relief. The relaxing background of surfers surfing, couples frolicking in the oceans and sunbathers bathing soothed my soul. I could look forward to tomorrow again. This new outlook lasted approximately seven minutes. As soon as Jackie's three loud, youthful and exuberant children came home they sent me back to square one. They were such an energetic bunch a couple of seconds in their company and you'd be shattered.

'They've been anticipating your arrival for days,' exclaimed Jackie.

The thrilled kids pounded their way upstairs and came bursting into my room. For the most part I was known as Uncle Nicholas to them. And then suddenly I'd become Father Christmas. Previously they may have smiled and said hi. However, with the added say I have over Xmas, they opted for giant hugs. The youngest of the trio Hannah leapt into my arms.

'Hello girls.'

They all looked at me sideways.

'Santa doesn't speak in that tone,' said Hannah.

'Yeah, be jollier, not so timid,' they insisted.

'Ho, ho, ho, young children. Better?' I wondered.

The girls squirmed, unhappy at my introduction. 'You come across insincere. More playful, less formal. Granddad had a casualness which compelled kids.'

These young ladies carried on criticising me from head to foot. It seemed everything I knew, said and did was wrong. If I'm to take notice of their instruction I'll walk, stand, talk and dress differently. The thing with kids is they have no filters or off button, because believe me my three nieces would have been muted. Their insults continued throughout dinner. Get this: even how I ate had flaws.

'You should chew roughly thirty times before swallowing. It'll help your digestion and prevent constipation,' said brainbox Hannah.

'That's quite enough, girls,' told Jackie.

I couldn't wait for their bedtime. Children between the ages of 6-13 require nine to eleven hours sleep to function at full strength. I received the treat of reading them a story. Not before they complained because I didn't do the voices properly.

'Daddy uses a variety of accents. You're using your normal droning speech.'

Infuriated by their constant bashing, I slammed the book shut; a cloud of dust shot into the air. Then I delivered my own bedtime tale. 'Once upon a time their lived three rude little girls who dissed Santa, so in return he struck their names off his list.'

It might've been mean of me, but their troubled faces saw who was truly boss.

'Santa's gotta know we're deeply sorry for any aggravation,' pleaded Hannah.

I departed with the notion if any hassle occurred, I'd cancel Christmas.

My newfound power allowed me not to worry so much.

I'd wrap up this mini vacation by visiting my brother, who left the freezing North Pole for the equally chilly Alaska. If you put us three siblings into categories Jackie is the brainy one, I'd be the sensible one and Terrell easily goes down as the fun one. He'd try anything once. As the years amassed

Terrell simmered somewhat; two rowdy boys and a wife had slowed his crazy lifestyle. That is until Christmas emerges. Alaska isn't a flashy state the likes of Florida, California or New York; it's humble by comparison and people lived modestly in logs cabins. Terrell home was impossible to miss. He began decorating his home in mid-November. During the Christmas period his home was visible from Mercury. One mile's worth of cable held up a thousand different lights. On his front lawn a huge inflatable Santa stood flapping its arms, and on the driveway three wise men travelled to a sleeping baby Jesus in a manger. Numerous elves, snowmen and reindeer littered his footpath. For me personally it was overkill and looked tacky. He'd received frequent complaints from annoyed neighbour. But instead of toning it down, Terrell amped up his Christmas spirit by purchasing a singing Santa Claus that on the hour every hour jigged about singing Jingle Bells.

Needless to say, he didn't exchange gifts with the locals. Inside his cabin the insane festive décor never wavered. I counted seven real life pine trees, tinsel was coiled around the banisters and tiny Santas hung from every light shade. He also sprayed white paint on windows sills to resemble snow.

'This is the season of goodwill to all God's men and women,' he greeted.

'Subtlety was never your speciality, was it?'

'Either do it big or don't do it at all,' said Terrell, offering me some delicious homemade eggnog.

The sweet vanilla extract and grated nutmeg flavour delighted my tummy. The warm sensation came from a wicked splash of potent rum. We reclined on his couch pouring glass after glass until we were rather wasted. Alcohol should come with a caution that consuming large quantities will open you up to some home truths you're not really ready for. He and I had devoured an entire batch of eggnog, which contained two litres of high-volume rum. We were watching some garbage cartoon when it parted for a quick advertisement break. What is it with commercial breaks any road? Don't you think they last longer than the programme nowadays? Let's forget that for a sec. Whilst adverts for toys, video games and food bombarded me, an annual advertisement struck Terrell deeply. A big red convoy of trucks rolled along a dark highway crossing a bridge, which then illuminated. Kids rejoiced for as they knew the holiday season was near. That notorious tune increased in the background as the Coca-Cola lorries entered the city bringing light to everything it passed.

Terrell begrudgingly sighed. 'This should all be mine.'

'What should be?' I asked.

He gulped a lot more eggnog and spoke from the heart. 'Christmas! The big job, of course. I'm rightfully deserving of being Santa Claus. I love Christmas in ways you can't imagine.'

'Santa goes to the first son,' I shrugged.

Terrell huffed; his intensity grew. Those normally fun-filled mint-green eyes glowed dangerously.

'You ain't got the heart for it. You proved it in Lapland. Some personalities don't suit certain jobs.'

The alcohol had a hold on us, and I returned with verbal fire. 'Meaning what, exactly, you punk?' I replied slurring.

Terrell's long fingers sternly clutched his glass; the force exerted shattered it. Fragments buried into his palm. 'You're a bum. You've hated Christmas from day one. That bah humbug mentality of yours will ruin the occasion.'

'Jealous twerp! For once I have something you want, and you cry foul. It's pathetic. You're an utter joke. Just can't stand my success.'

'Jealously? Success? That's rich bro,' he spewed.

In fiery arguments you shouldn't let the opposition have the final word. Even when you are wrong, keep arguing for argument's sake.

'I got it all, the lavish pad at the North Pole, the power, glory and the adoration of billions. How do you equate? Crappy two bed log cabin, average job, and a devastating notion you'll never ever be Father Claus.' Game set and match; the dispute was securely won.

Unfortunately, Terrell had home court advantage, so inevitably booted my backside out.

# CHAPTER 8

## The Toy

Finally, I caught a break; a motel downtown had a late cancellation and slashed their original fee in half. The drab room missed the whole Christmas theme. All it contained was one single bed with clingfilm thin quilts and pillows which felt stuffed with rocks, a nightstand and a bedside lamp. The absence of Xmas cheer came as a wonderful interval. I tried to let my mind stray away from the mounting chaos. As I nodded off, instead of dreaming I flashed back to a time where my hatred for this ungodly season begun. Perhaps my fondness of Christmas dissipated more so over time, but as for the initial bitterness we'll have go to the year 1989.

In 1989 a lot of things were occurring in the world: for example, Germany dismantled the Berlin Wall. None of this meant anything to me. I was ten years young and still wet behind the ears, too naïve to understand how the Christmas machine operated. Father had his best Xmas production yet, being way ahead of schedule. This period can only be described as the peak of his peak. He commanded the elves

with consummate ease, and they obeyed orders to his speci-
fication. I wished back then I'd studied Father's mannerism
on how to interact with his crew, then my reign wouldn't be
as turbulent. On a physical note his bones didn't ache, his
hair wasn't grey, and he was in mighty fine shape. For us kids
we enjoyed dear time with our parents. We were in rare company; seeing father during the Christmas melee almost never
occurred. I don't know if I've explained properly about what
it's really like being the son of Father Claus. You'd probably
guess Santa as your daddy is awesome. Awesome? Well, perhaps on opposite day. Get that stupid idea out of your head.
The kids of Santa suffer most. Whilst we were on his list, we
weren't exactly priorities; our names usually lingered close to
the bottom. Sometimes we settled for whatever faulty gifts
were left. We received odd-shaped Lego, dry Play-doh that
was virtually impossible to mould and action figures missing
limbs. I remember one year playing with a Scalextric which
caused frequent electrical shocks.

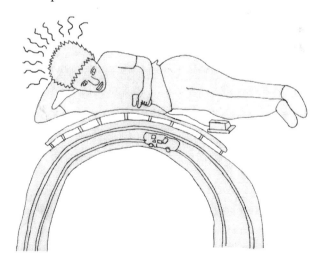

59

If I stand approximately four feet from the microwave a zapping tingle shoots through the right side of my body. I'm confident in saying the sole present I got for Christmas is the task of servicing the entire world's need for gifts. I'm one lucky chap. Sorry, I'm beginning to throw myself a pity party. Before Father went on his death-defying travels, he'd always find a couple of minutes to gather us all together. He'd commence by saying something so profound and chilling.

'There aren't many guarantees in life.' He paused, gazing blatantly at me. 'Every time I take to the sky there's a strong chance it's my last.'

Only now do those words register in my brain; the sky has capabilities of being a fatal foe. Jackie used to get terribly upset any time he left. She'd cry for the whole day, staying up all night until his return.

'I love you to pieces and since I've got myself a spare day before my trip, what do you guys want to do?'

'The choice is yours, dad,' we conceded.

Over the November and December months father religiously remained locked up in his workshop. He was itching for something fresh and interesting. What surprised me was what he considered fresh and interesting we considered tedious and ordinary. 'I'd love to go shopping and see Christmas from a different viewpoint.'

So, like many families, we wrapped up snugly and braved the Christmas rush. Father learned very soon that people during the Christmasmania are rude, arrogant and sometimes violent. Before we even entered the shopping-centre getting a parking spot alone was tough. Crazy customers jammed their vehicles in any available space and folks with able bodies slotted their cars in disabled locations. Two men paralysed from the waist down threw haymakers, knocking each other onto the ground. Both guys furiously wrestled to gain the upper hand; they were quite agile for men unable to use their legs.

Father observed their aggressive manner. 'Unbelievable! I thought people were happier this time of year.'

'It's the last week of shopping. Anything can and will go down. Stay on guard. No foolish antics and whatever unfolds don't lose contact,' informed mother.

The thing you gotta realise is back in the 80s no internet existed, which meant no online shopping. Amazon or eBay! Give over, everyone shopped the good old-fashioned way. High Streets were battlegrounds, market stalls were warzones and stores were the frontline. It was sheer unorganised carnage. Black Friday doesn't have a lick on the 80s Christmas heat. Due to the fact this was the last weekend prior to Xmas people were extra stressed. The shopping centre was in disarray; naked mannequins lounged in windows, shelves were practically empty, and parents dragged kids from outlet stores carrying half a dozen bags.

A man dressed as Santa offered gift wrapping services.

'Imposter,' frowned dad.

'Have you seen enough yet?' declared mother.

'Nah, I want to get into the thick of it.' Father waltzed towards the busiest shop.

I recall this shop so well from its store clerk's uniform, giant red letters displaying the name Games, Gadgets & Goodies, a department store for all no matter how rich or poor. Giddy children eyed up expensive items and frustrated parents spent their Christmas bonuses to keep them quiet.

'Mommy, can I get this?'

'Daddy, can I have that?' yelled several spoiled kids.

Father chuckled as a child tugged his mother's arms.

'Should've been nice and Santa wouldn't have crossed you off his list, Roberto,' he whispered.

Roberto's face froze, absolutely freaked out by a stranger knowing his name.

Allow me to clarify; these children begging for gifts are the naughty ones. You can tell just by how they act, screaming, demanding and not listening. There's a system in place that filters out any child who isn't behaving and instantly their Christmas lists are rejected and sent back. Certain silly parents can't bear their kids going present-less, so instead take the list and frantically attempt to tick off every toy.

Anyway, gadgets were flying off displays and shelves faster than employees could stock them. The mad scramble intensified when the store manager made an incredible announcement. He stood on the counter as a tug of war for the final remaining gifts ensued.

'Attention folk! May I have your attention please.'

The desperate group halted fighting for a brief moment.

'It's with great pleasure I reveal a last-minute shipment of this years must have has arrived.'

Silence cast suspense over the customers, employees and security guards, who were working relentlessly breaking up conflict.

'The Sega Genesis is here!' he said brazenly.

For those of you only aware of PlayStation and Xbox being kings of the game console, prior to the high spec we see today another Japanese manufacturer had children obsessed. The Genesis wasn't their first or last console, but it's the one I desired most. Games such as Mortal Kombat and Sonic would come to define its illustrious run. Every man and boy on the entire planet fantasised about owning it.

An epic wave of noise blasted our eardrums and hundreds of customers shoved, nudged and barged, racing to the counter. We took a backward step, not wanting to be crushed. Although the console had a R.R.P; Recommended Retail Price, cunning consumers brought two. They'd keep one and double the price of the other. Within seconds of his announcement the Game, Gadgets & Goodies manager declared.

'In deep sympathy the Sega Genesis is officially sold out. Our stores in New York, San Francisco and Dallas still have limited stock.'

Determined customers wrote down store addresses, rang and reserved the console and then drove for hours.

'That's what the fuss is all about, a black box? You know I've been making them for three months straight,' said dad.

My brother and I were totally flabbergasted. The boundless enjoyment children experienced compelled us to ask a man with an inside track.

'Dad, I know you always say we should be grateful for our blessings. And I am truly. I also would be overly grateful if a Sega Genesis landed in my stocking,' I suggested.

'Yeah, I heard you're the man to speak to,' added Terrell.

'I won't confirm or deny anything,' he slyly shrugged. 'But let it be known your request is being considered.'

Usually father knocked down our gift ideas automatically. On this occasion his noncommittal answer felt as good as a yes.

Terrell and I were elated; maybe too elated. That night as the moon simmered over the sprawling white metropolis of the North Pole Terrell kept fidgeting above me. His bunk bed rattled. We were only three sleeps from Christmas and with each passing day we grew more anxious.

'Less than seventy hours to go,' spurted Terrell.

'Are we gonna go through this every night?'

He rolled to the edge of his bed, leaning over the side. The moon lit up his gleaming face. He had these gigantic dimples you could swim in and a smile that could crack the meanest of men. 'You're right, let's do something about it.'

'Yeah, remain composed and wait until Christmas,' I responded.

'The anticipation is unhealthy. I can't sleep. We must act.'

'Don't be daft, Terrell; father essentially promised us a Sega Genesis.'

My brother was an act first, think later person. He quickly hopped out of bed grabbed his winter coat, scarf, gloves and boots. 'Are you coming?'

Regrettably, I followed his lead. We gingerly made our way outside, avoiding the spotlight which detected movement. It was a small distance from the main house to dad's workshop. Terrell and I kept really low on all fours, so our snow prints looked as though an animal made them. With the valuable equipment stored inside the workshop father locked up after himself.

'Great, it's locked. Let's go back,' I said urgently.

'You'd like that, wouldn't you?' Terrell searched a few rocks that lay on the ground, unearthing a spare key.

We entered the workshop. The place was pristinely clean; all the presents were neatly stacked and tightly wrapped with gift tags for every child.

'Where do we even begin?' I said dumbfounded.

'These are outgoing presents; we needn't sweat over them. Upstairs is where personal gifts are.'

I had my suspicions Terrell had done this before. He knew exactly where to go far too easily. Behind a tree several presents resided. We didn't bother to read the tags because of the Genesis' shape. Our eyes were fixated on the golden wrapping paper and sparkled off its reflection.

'Now we know we should head home.'

'Not so fast, Nick. Just one glimpse,' said Terrell carefully peeling away part of the Sellotape.

'And how do we wrap it back?' I wondered.

'Please, I've been doing since I could crawl,' he proclaimed.

Terrell and I were mesmerised we'd actually got something that wasn't a cast off. He expertly resealed the wrapper without making a crease and we crept back to bed.

Christmas day sure took its sweet time; nevertheless, we exchanged gifts at noon. Father brought over a familiar box in scintillating gold.

'Terrell, Nick, this is yours.'

'I wonder what it could be,' cheekily winked Terrell.

We simultaneously ripped the paper away discovering a demoralising, heartbreaking and outright depressing gift.

'Another beat-down, off-brand Scalextric,' I complained.

Terrell's dimples sunk deeper; his smile faded as tears forged a path down his cheeks. 'I saw with my own two eyes, a Sega Genesis,' he let slip.

'Well that's what you get for snooping,' Dad fumed.

'But dad,' we cried.

'But nothing, I got eyes everywhere,' he told us sternly. From then on Xmas could go to hell.

# CHAPTER 9

## What the Elf is Going On

The Lapland mess was as old as stale bread. At the airport nobody glanced or offered an unkind word. I spoke to mother and she informed me the harassing reporters had left. It seemed as though things were running smoothly again. The flight suffered no delays, and my scheduled arrival was bang on time. Whilst in the air I met a lovely young flight stewardess who recognised me from the television. Her name tag read Molly.

'Looking forward to Christmas?' she asked politely.

'Looking forward to it being over, you mean,' I groaned.

She tied her hair back, exposing her beautiful face, a cute button nose, engaging brown eyes and skin that bore a resemblance to silk. 'You're the face of Christmas, so mighty and powerful.'

'Am I now?'

'Think about it, who else has such an influence? A president, a king, perhaps a dictator?' Her enlightening words moved me.

We continued talking as I ordered my inflight meal. Molly's attention never faltered; she acted as if we were the only two people on the plane.

We chatted and laughed; she possessed a killer snorting giggle. 'Oh my, how shameful,' she covered her mouth using her left hand which displayed no wedding ring.

'Don't be ashamed; our unique quirks make us who we are. It's cute,' I encouraged. She blushed, rather flattered; then to show her gratitude fiddled with the seating arrangements, bumping me up to first class. There the wealth was exposed for all to view; passengers received complimentary beverages, had comfy neck pillows and noise cancelling headphones for a movie of their choosing.

Little did I know it then, but I had met the future Mrs Claus. It's almost laughable how situations unfold. If the Lapland debacle wasn't a major obstacle my detour would have been unnecessary and then fate wouldn't have led me to the amazing Molly. That's life people; behind every tragedy is ultimately a blessing. We exchanged contact details, you know, the norm: Twitter, Snapchat, Instagram and Facebook.

Roughly about midday I rolled up to the North Pole on a snowmobile dashing through the snow. I didn't expect a rousing welcoming committee but what I got was colder than the climate we resided in. The dismayed reindeer's antlers drooped, and they stomped their hooves in irritation. I'm not fluent in reindeer; however, by the looks of them they wanted no part of my return. The single person I relied on being delirious about my homecoming was mother. She baked me a welcome back pie with stewed beef, carrots, mushrooms and onions. There is no comparison to mother's cooking.

'My baby's home,' she gushed, grabbing my cheeks.

'Stop, you're smothering me,' I said, perturbed.

She eagerly sat at the table, her hands propping up her head. 'So, other than the obvious blunder, how was your maiden outing as Father Claus? Did it live up to expectation?'

'It was what it was,' I casually replied, digging into the puff pastry.

Mothers have their own clever way of making you open up without much effort. 'Tell mom,' she spoke softly. As kids this voice disarmed us and as adults still controlled me. I'd promised myself not to mention Molly and the next minute mom knew more about her than I did. Mom's facial features changed; her eyebrows rose, the eyes squinted, and her lips curled. 'If you want to impress her, invite her for Christmas. What's more festive than a real Christmas with Santa and his family? Your father did it and won me over.'

'I'll give it some thought,' I said, pouring water on the idea.

69

After I washed mom's delicious pie down with a cup of tea, I ventured across the footpath to an all too quiet workshop. Something appeared odd. Walking towards the front door, I noticed only my Wellingtons left marks in the snow, the blinds were closed, and the lights weren't on either. Upon entering the workshop, I observed a room exactly the way I remembered ten days ago. Dust collected on work surfaces, presents that were supposed to be wrapped, tagged and bagged laid unfinished.

'Those devious, dirty elves,' I seethed.

Apparently, my mini break was extended to employees too. I went barmy; a torrid sensation burnt behind my eyes and I found it hard to restrain my anger. How could they? How dare they? I thought to myself. I took a page out of Terrell's book and decided to confront the slacking workforce. With my short walk to their residence I grew increasingly annoyed; my blood bubbled under the surface. I hammered the door aggressively to a point where I worried the hinges wouldn't last. A curtain in the living room flicked signalling they were awake.

'You ratbags, come out now!' I demanded.

BANG! BANG! BANG! The door near enough imploded on itself. I'd weakened the frame and structure with my constant pounding. When anger comes over you—and I mean real anger, not someone calling you a silly name you undoubtedly lose it. Acting out of spite can only lead to future complication.

Ever so slowly what was left of their front door opened. Fletcher, an elf who'd recently taken up the responsibility of leader, greeted me with crust still in his eyes and in a long navy-blue robe. 'Nick! Good to have you home.'

'Where do you get your arrogance from?' I screamed.

'Arrogance from my mom, height from my dad. That guy still owes me a few inches,' he joked.

'Look, I assumed you'd have the presents virtually finished by now, and yet production came to a standstill.'

He gazed at me as if I was nothing to no one. 'You know what happens when you assume things. You make an a-s-s out of you and me.' Fletcher had no reason to be intimidated. I needed them more than they needed me. He cockily approached me till our shoes were touching; this now put us nose to navel. 'I'll expect you to fix the door upon exiting.'

His disobedience stung. Somehow, he'd made himself the victim.

'You listen; until otherwise informed, I'm the boss,' I sniped.

'Keep telling yourself that, you might believe it.'

Fletcher had undermined my authority for the last time. 'You think you're really something special,' I said, nudging him backwards.

'Me? I'm a simple old sod doing as I'm told.'

A loud outburst of laughter resounded from the living area. Their wild giggles tipped me into maniac mode. The red mist didn't only descend, it consumed my soul. I was having a problem breathing; a blood vessel popped in my nostril, dripping blood onto my favourite white shirt.

'Calm down lad, I gather you're under immense stress,' rationalised Fletcher, pulling out a packet of tissues.

'You guys aren't making it easy,' I said, pinching my nose and tilting my head back.

'To be frank you haven't been good to us either, firing whoever, whenever. How can we trust an unstable boss?'

'I'm trying to run an efficient operation.'

'Well, reducing the taskforce doesn't aid efficiency, now does it?' Fletcher smugly patted my thigh.

He had me in retreat, asking questions of myself. It's said that in life you get in what you give out and maybe these elves weren't rebelling but requesting fair treatment. Then another antagonising level of chuckles tortured my eardrums. It reminded me why I was initially so infuriated. 'I'm a lot things but born yesterday ain't one of them.'

I barged into the lounge where his confidants were held up watching the classic Xmas film Home Alone and sharing a giant bowl of popcorn. Well, giant to them anyway. My appearance did little to deter their fun.

'Oh, aye up, gaffer's here,' declared an Elf mockingly.

Some elves pretended to clean up, moving an ashtray from one disgusting area to an equally filthy location. They lived like slobs. Bugs would have rather the freezing climate than enter this abyss. Several different wallpapers were poorly pasted on the walls, toxic green fungus covered their skirting boards, and the stifling scent of cigarettes polluted every room. In movies you get a very elegant, refined and well-mannered image of Santa's little helpers, which in my non-biased opinion couldn't be further from reality. They are ghastly, repulsive and uncooperative people. Rude, abrasive, destructive, hateful, cunning, disrespectful . . . I could go on forever describing them.

'We all know how hectic Christmas is. Why aren't you guys at work?'

'Technically speaking, you never left us any instructions. As loyal employees we felt uncomfortable and missed your stupendous leadership,' said Fletcher.

The entire elf community held their lips together, attempting not to chuckle.

'Spin it however you want, we're all knee deep in the muck,' I yelled.

'As far as I'm concerned, if Christmas Day sucks worldwide the criticism lands at your doorstep, not ours. After all, the boss takes credit for everything and hardly does anything,' proclaimed Fletcher's sidekick.

They had me in a quandary. Should I keep poking the bear and hope they fold or compromise for a greater purpose? Nah, I chose the former.

'Yo, Nicky boy, shift your fat butt, I'm trying to watch the box,' insulted an elf.

'Sorry, allow me to assist your viewing pleasure.' Incensed, I prised the flat screen from its wall bracket screws and all.

'Don't do anything stupid,' pleaded an elf.

'Little Nicky can't help himself, he's as stupid as stupid can be,' blasted Fletcher.

'Little Nicky? In your world I'm Goliath.' I hurled the device out the window.

SMASH!

The glass shattered. Debris scattered everywhere, wounding some elves sitting below the window. A minor part of me harboured sympathy, but what's done is done.

The talkative bunch was stunned to a petrified silence.

'Let it be clear; I don't fudge about. Now get ready for some strenuous graft. You've got ten minutes,' I brutally ordered

# CHAPTER 10

## The Strike

I'd painted myself into a corner the likes many villains can't escape. If I apologise, I'm perceived as vulnerable, a push-over; however, in standing firm I'm callous. Either course I can't win. The elves had their own dilemma whether to rise or fall. I curiously awaited their reaction inside the warmth of my workshop. Ten minutes came went and went again. I kept anticipating a demoralised Fletcher and his posse to amble in, surrendering to a high power. Seconds crept to minutes and minutes merged into hours. I peeked out through a slit in the blinds; their home resumed a look of normality barring the smashed front window and partially functional door. A glare of divine sunlight squirted through crack in a cloud shining directly above the Elf's home. After three hours twenty-one minutes and seventeen seconds (not that I'm counting) Fletcher and one or two of his top boys stood on their front porch. They menacingly scowled at the workshop. Like that's supposed to scare me. I had eaten meals and taken dumps bigger than them. If they expected me to grovel in desperation on bended knees, they've got a better chance of reaching an average height. Am I making too many short gags? How belittling of me.

Fletcher and his crew discussed their predicament extensively; every once in a while, he'd make hand motions towards the workshop. I figured something heinous would transpire by the way their in-depth conversation went. Each sentence seemed to get them angrier. The elves weren't only annoyed at me but had conflict amongst their gang too. I slightly pulled the door ajar. I laid flat on the floor, straining my eyes to observe their moving lips and stretched my ears to listen in.

'His back's braced against the wall. We got him on the rocks. Let him sweat it; he'll have little option but to concede to our every demand,' concluded Fletcher.

Hamilton, his deputy, scrunched up his nose, unsure about Fletcher's wait and see approach. 'I say we show a united front, go straight for the jugular.'

'Nah, it'll set in shortly. He's alone without a hope and prayer. Christmas will be an utter shambolic washout. You just hold tight.'

'What if you're incorrect? What if he is as stubborn, foolish and dim-witted as we predict?'

'Which he is,' responded Fletcher. *Ouch, that hurts.*

'Then he'll let Christmas go by the wayside and regroup next year with an entirely new cast of staff.'

Fletcher scratched his head as though rubbing off a scratch card with his fingernail. He contemplated Hamilton's stance and appreciated how limited their opportunity was. 'Organise the crew; it's gonna be a long night,' he commanded.

Hamilton ran inside calling his colleagues outside.

I wouldn't describe my emotions then as frightened, although there was definitely a sense of apprehension.

During a half hour span plenty of upheaval unfolded. Elves rushed in and out their home. Fletcher directed who did what, his masculine voice bellowing instructions. I heard cutting, gluing, taping, hammering and gunfire, a nail gun that is. The commotion halted as quickly as it started. These elves were so at home with one another it took a matter of minutes for them to synchronise.

As a show of resilience, I departed the workshop. A vague stillness consumed the atmosphere; the gentle breeze that often blew subsided. I crossed my arms, inflated my chest and placed the sternest of frowns on my face. In business this is known as posturing, presenting a notion of invincibility when underneath you're clueless.

Fletcher, Hamilton and their warriors marched in tandem. They brought signs with my face attached; banners included disturbing slurs and a dummy wearing a dunce cap labelled "Thick Nick." They'd really gone to H.A.M, expressing their displeasure by sticking my picture on a dartboard with darts stuck in my skull. A vengeful spite carried their savage, disparaging chants. The peaceful North Pole turned into battlefield; elves rallied and ranted, burning their God-awful green uniforms in a metal barrel. Black smoke filled the air, making the whole scene dramatic. Behind the ravenous flames, elves screamed creative off-colour remarks.

'Nick! Nick is a stupid twit. He's brain-dead, smells and that's only the half of it,' they harmoniously belted. 'He's also fat, balding and an ugly git.'

Untalented, fat, ugly? I'll give you that. Balding on the other hand I'm not quite sure. Losing hair is nothing to ridicule someone over. Baldness will affect fifty per cent of men before fifty. Sorry male population. I checked my reflection in the workshop window, discovering they weren't wrong. The stresses of Santa had activated the receding process and silver strands flashed amongst my black barnet. My eyebrows were invaded with greys too. Was I morphing into my old man already?

Fletcher conducted the strike like a masterful conductor. He waved his stubby arms, telling them when to increase their chants. The hatred spewed; their voices strained in passion. It seemed as though the world was against me. My father must've loved this since I'd shunned all his wisdom. Moment by moment the likelihood of us meeting our Christmas deadline significantly reduced. The elves might be diminutive in stature, but they were powerful in song.

I slotted my index fingers inside my ears, pretending not to hear. Straight away it proved I was rattled. They came closer, bringing a new degree of intensity. They surrounded me, circling like swarming bees. 'Nick! Nick is a stupid twit. He's brain-dead, smells and that's only the half it.' They repeated viciously.

My nerves were shaken to some extent. Fletcher and Co had knocked the stuffing out of me. My head said concede whilst my heart told me to stand up like a durable tower.

As each elf rotated, they cast their judgement.

'Idiot!'

'Fool!'

'Buffoon!'

'I know you are, but what am I?' I retaliated.

'Brilliant. Good one. How long did it take you to come up with that?' criticised Hamilton.

Nightfall was arriving; the sun had gradually drifted off. A developing moon occupied the dreary sky yet still a dozen elves relentlessly antagonised. The chant that did the most harm wasn't witty or clever; it simply held a lot of truth. 'You're not as good as your dad! You're not as good as your dad!' The echo lingered indefinitely.

It's a devastating statement no successor wants to believe. There and then a surge of inadequacy prevailed. Father Claus' suit was a huge one to fill. Have you ever worn your dad's slippers? Then you know what I'm talking about. Thoughts of disappointing a historical dynasty riddled my mind. Here and now I learnt a valuable life lesson; some things are bigger than your own agenda. Christmas being one of them. I collared Fletcher, who promptly silenced his raucous crew.

'What will it take to squash our differences?' I asked.

Fletcher smiled so hard his eyes closed. Hamilton handed him a sealed brown envelope.

The elves eagerly stared as I opened their list of demands. I nodded at certain suggestions in agreement, mainly fix the door, window and buy them a new television. However, upon scrolling the last few bullet points I gauged they didn't just want equality, but to humiliate me as well.

I must wear an elf costume at all times

Clean their home from top to bottom (including washing and ironing)

Pay for their annual summer holiday

Refer to them as associates rather than helpers

'You're nuts to think I'd agree to these terms,' I huffed.

Fletcher tilted his head up; a sinister glower comprised his bulging nose, puffy eyes and clenched gnashers. 'Those aren't requests. They're outright necessities.'

'Please, I ain't anybody's whipping boy. So, bring it on.' I simulated, wiping my bum with the letter before tossing it aside.

If the elves were miffed already, my disregard to even negotiate achieved a new degree of disgust.

Hamilton pushed his blond hair behind his ears. 'Stubbornness and youth are synonymous.'

Elves began to retreat, sensing their strike was fool's gold. They dismantled the plaques, posters and life-sized dummy.

'That's right run away you cowards,' I yelled. 'Start working now and all is forgiven.'

Fletcher and his disenchanted workers huddled together like an American football team designing an offensive play. Fletcher kneeled, putting one knee in the deep snow. Their whispers were muffled by rasping winds rifling through the North Pole. Hamilton broke the huddle and three elves splintered off, sprinting out of view.

'What will it be?' I asked.

'Gotta give you a big fat no. You won't accept our compromise so accept our punishment.' Fletcher maintained a twenty-metre gap between us.

'Oh yeah, you and what army? A great big man beats twelve little men seven days to Sunday.'

The elves laughed profusely.

'Great! Great? You give yourself far too much praise,' replied Hamilton, receiving the thumbs up from his colleagues.

'Come prove me wrong,' I said removing my jacket and tightening both fists.

Fletcher wagged his finger. 'We aren't gonna fight you.'

'Thought so. All talk no walk. Pathetic.'

'Just because we aren't violent doesn't mean we don't understand the rules of combat.'

His mysterious words only baffled and perplexed me. 'Say what now?'

'You have enemies in the animal kingdom too.'

'Now!' ordered Hamilton.

Three elves rapidly pulled the chains off the reindeer's hut. The door flew wide open. Eight ill-tempered brutes sought vengeance. A tremendous growl rumbled as the four-legged terrors were unleashed. The tragic death of Randolph hadn't been avenged as yet. A worried sweat oozed, collecting in my boots. The confidence I generally displayed liquefied like a snowman in eighty-degree weather.

The reindeer brashly approached with their heads down and antlers up. In the glamorous moonlight their antlers glimmered and resembled several piercing kitchen knives.

'Guys, can we discuss this like jolly good chaps?' I begged.

'Now he wants to chat. How convenient.' Fletcher coldly looked me dead in my eyes. 'The time for talking is over. Your reign was brief with deer results.'

His elves trundled off, ignoring his dreadful joke.

I clumped and balled together large quantities of snow. 'Get back, you vile scum,' I barked, launching my assault. The snowballs had no significant impact. They crept further forward, watching me twitch. A machine gun wouldn't have prevented their advances. One of the reindeer particularly close to the late great Randolph scrapped the patient stalking tactic and bolted. He galloped ahead grunting insanely. His allies joined the onslaught. All I witnessed was a flurry of white dust charging into my personal space. Instinctively my feet took leave, scampering through the snowy land.

The evil reindeer were faster than I thought; on a couple of occasions I felt their spiky antlers dig into my side. Their swift sideswipes were alarming wake-up calls. I kept on progressing even as my feet got heavier and chest got tighter. When in immense danger your whole body goes into survival mode. You think clearer. Your actions become more deliberate. Strategically I led them into the forest, a location I knew better than anyone. Terrell and I were practically raised in the forest building dens. The combinations of trees, bushes and high grass allowed me a perfect hiding place. I stooped down behind a hedge, peeking at the reindeer's shadows in the moonlit sky. They sniffed around, trying to get a whiff of a trail. I'd envisioned them doing that and covered myself in dirt. Soon the reindeer departed, groaning at not having honoured Randolph. Inside the woods, amongst the plethora of shrubs, lay a narrow wooden footpath father forbade us from crossing. Well, he isn't here now.

# CHAPTER 11

## New Way of Life

Why is it certain activities that once had you frightened turn out to be anticlimactic? I tentatively walked the path, looking over both shoulders, thinking the dangerous reindeer or despicable elves may return to finish the job. I was jittery and hearing any creak and squeak made my heart frantically tick. I stuck my arms out in front of me, expecting something to imminently attack. Branches whipped together in the wind, shaking freezing snow onto my body. I shuddered. The path finally merged into another lacklustre scene of vacant land encased with white snow. What a hype job. All of Father's bluster; stay away from the path, there's an unknown killer who dwells there. The only distinct difference between our home and this area is the snow. To most humans snow is snow, white, a powdery texture unless you clump it together. Actually there are at least six separate types of snow crystals. Star, Dendrite, Columns, Plates, Columns with capped plates and Needles. They are formed in all kinds of temperatures and I'm boring you. The snow I ambled across felt sturdy like concrete. It had little give and hardly crunched when trampled on.

I walked as far as my feet would take me; after all, there was nothing left for me. Father had practically disowned me; my brother lived in envy, the reindeer and elves you know the story. Oh yes, Santa had fallen on hard times. I entertained the idea of changing my name and simply running away for good. The night closed in further. An imposing moon graced me as I strolled, stranded on a road to nowhere. A colder, more potent breeze flowed, ruffling my bloodstained t-shirt. I folded and squeezed my arms together, maintaining whatever body heat remained; my nipples were so erect you could've hung coats off them. Without shelter I was guaranteed to freeze to death. On the bright side my untimely death would see Terrell promoted, Randolph's fatal accident avenged, and the elves wouldn't be so disruptive. Perhaps life will be better once I'm gone.

No, I shouldn't think that way. I still have a lot to offer. As I carried on trudging, I skittishly scanned the highest mountain and lowest of valleys seeking a place to sleep. Kind of like Mary and Joseph, just a morbid version. As hollow and alone as I'd become, something inter-  nally wouldn't let up. I'm not one for miracles but a single star shone. The intense spark attracted me. It acted as a chaperone, guiding me to an abandoned igloo.

Upon tapping the roof, I assumed one of two things, it was empty and whoever built this took pride. The smooth snow bricks were perfectly comprised with zero cracks or crumbles. I crawled through the narrow tunnel where I'd hunkered down until morning.

That following morning, I heard chatter but wasn't able to communicate.

'Is he dead? He seems frozen solid,' said a womanly voice.

'Could be hypothermia; he isn't appropriately dressed for this environment. His clothes are ringing wet,' assessed a dominant male figure. He crouched over my violently shivering body to fully diagnosis me. 'He's breathing, albeit shallowly. His skin's paler than the snow he rests on.'

'Will he survive?' asked an innocent-sounding child.

'That's for him to decide. All I can do is follow procedure.'

Although medical attention is recommended if ever a friend, family member or even stranger shows symptoms of hypothermia, you should immediately move the person inside, remove all their damp clothes (not a good day to go commando), dry them and then wrap the patient in towels, blankets and robes. In extreme cases say a million Hail Marys too.

He'd wrapped me up tighter than a professionally made burrito. Within a four hour span my core temperature began climbing to its thirty-seven degrees optimum. The erratic shake was gone, and the sensation returned to my fingers and toes. I dusted the ice from my frosted beard and eyebrows. A stunning sunshine lavishly patrolled the December morning, showering us in luxurious rays. Last night, casting my eyes over the land, I thought I'd stumbled across a lonesome igloo. Today I recognised my mistake. I'd entered a community of Inuits. Inuits is the politically correct term for those who live in Arctic regions. You're not the only one who thought they were called Eskimos. I'll confess in my ignorance I didn't bother to research either. A variety of almost identical igloos were plotted in rows each house had specific number like a home address.

'Daddy, he is alive,' squealed a little girl with beads in her hair.

Her parents squinted vaguely in surprise and partly in hesitation. They grabbed their daughter before she rushed to me. Living in a community where everyone knows everyone this girl never fretted.

'What did we tell you about outsiders?' said her mother sternly.

The girl innocently shrugged. She remembered but instead played dumb to avoid a harsh punishment.

'I have no intention of harming you,' I proclaimed, easing their reservations.

The lady lowered her hoodie; she rapidly swivelled her head like an owl. 'A serial killer would say the same thing.'

'I'm Nicholas Claus Jr. I used to live over yonder.'

'My name's Yura, that's my daughter Yuka and the gentlemen who covered your bare backside is my husband Miki.' She loosened her defence.

My filthy clothes were hand-washed and now dried over their fire. Ah, how nice of them. I kneeled down by her side as she sliced some sort of white meat into chunks.

'I can't express my gratefulness. If you didn't arrive when you had I'd have perished. I'll repay you in any way you see fit,' I emotionally stated.

'Your wellbeing is payment enough, young man,' proclaimed Miki. Miki is a traditional name in their native tongue; it means small. If he's small, I'd hate to see big. Miki towered over me. He had arms to rival the Michelin Man, a buff chest and legs that wouldn't look out of place on a Mr

Olympia stage. You could sense a mild nature from him even though he looked as if he could wrestle a polar bear. Beside the impressive physique Miki possessed seniority around the camp. Due to his favourable standing I had zero qualms for being a so-called outsider. Who's to say what's an insider or an outsider? Aren't we all human?

Yuka was fascinated by viewing someone she perceived as different. 'Don't have a family?'

'Quit asking questions, missy,' hissed Yura.

'It's quite all right.' I saw her enthusiasm as adorable. 'Yuka, I'll let you in on a very private secret.'

Her cheeks flooded in colour, Yuka's eyes expanded so wide her eyelashes and eyelids disappeared. 'Tell me! I'm fantastic at keeping things to myself.'

Yura and Miki equally sniggered knowing that not to be true.

'Well, a short while ago, I was Father Christmas.'

Yuka cringed to think the partially clothed man curled up in a frigid ball last night could once have been the almighty Santa Claus. 'So where did it go wrong?'

'How rude! Apologise now,' yelled Yura, tossing whatever fleshy substance into a boiling pot.

Yuka instantly apologised.

'It's a sore spot,' I said.

Miki fixed me a plate of what I want to say is shark stew. Large white pieces floated on top of a gooey liquid. He extended an offer in solidarity. 'You're free to join us here provided you learn the Inuit lifestyle.'

'I'm a lump of clay. Mould me.'

My Inuit learning curve was a steep one. Miki introduced me to a simpler way of existing. They lived a self-sufficient life, eating what they killed. Coats were made out of various animal furs. Animal lovers say what you will. The warmth generated from a wolf or polar bear's fur can't be replicated. Miki took to teaching me the art of ice fishing in a hurry. He'd promised his community I wouldn't be a burden. This meant my evolution had to be fast tracked. We walked to a nearby lake which remained buried beneath seven inches of solid ice. He rested his tool bag forged from walrus skin on the ice. Again, animal worshippers, quit your yabbering. Aren't you a hypocrite sitting there on your leather sofa? In any case, he gave me something called a hand auger. Its design reminded me of a corkscrew between the twirled metal end and flat handle; it was basically a carbon copy on a magnified scale.

'There's three key components to a fulfilling life. Food, shelter and love,' preached Miki.

'If I snag a fish today, I'll be one to the good,' I said, faintly grinning.

'Let's not bog ourselves down in negativity. The mammals will become spooked. Now begin to drill until the ice breaks.'

I duly twisted the handle clockwise as the metal drill scratched and scraped the icy surface. Ice flakes sprung up hitting me in the face. My forearms burnt furiously. I could see now what created Miki's sculpted physique. The energy draining boredom ceased when the ice gave out and freezing water splashed us both.

'We're in. Well done, Nick.'

We eagerly pitched our rods and waited and waited furthermore. Soon it became evident the fishes weren't willing to play. Slightly pessimistic I retrieved our equipment and packed for home.

'Ice fishing is a hit and miss business,' Miki explained. 'One day you hit the motherlode, then weeks elapse without a single tug on your line. You shouldn't be discouraged.'

'But all that work for no pay off seems pointless,' I replied downbeat.

'Such is life. Listen don't hang your head or slump those shoulders; failures happen. Plus, you've got an igloo to construct.'

I floundered, dreading the prospect of assembling my own igloo. 'They look super complicated.'

'There's nothing to it, trust me. Dab of snow here, splodge of snow there, bing, bang, bosh,' reassured Miki as we arrived home.

Inuit people aren't ones to speak just for the sake of it. Miki's clan had already plotted out a spacious section of real estate. Next to the hard-packed snow were the essential items I required to produce my igloo. A snow shovel, carving knife, two long sticks and a piece of string. I gawked at each object with a quaint unfamiliarity.

'Hurry up chap; nightfall is pending,' shouted an impatient fellow.

A tense atmosphere dangled above me like a stormy cloud.

'Stab and circle,' hinted Miki.

'No coaching,' bellowed a husky voice.

Miki triggered my memory; his guidance started to pay off big style. I planted one stick in the centre of my land then tied a string to the bottom of both sticks. I scuffed out a symmetrical circular line for the outer wall. Once satisfied, I picked up the snow knife, carving large blocks of snow from inside of the newly formed diameter. Now I had a foot-deep trench work began composing my first layer. I firmly levelled down the snow around the rim and strategically placed each block. I made sure the initial rows of bricks were sloped inwards to give me that dome shape. To plug any gaps I used loose snow, gently patting it into odd spots. As I went on, I carefully studied where my next block should go. The higher I got the smaller and lighter the blocks became.

Miki joyfully monitored my detailed placement. 'Taught him everything he knows,' he bragged.

As my igloo skills flourished so did my coolness. I causally whistled and skipped, digging a hole for my entrance. Most first-timers go for a humdrum square opening. However, I opted for a sophisticated archway. Within no time what-soever I cut and positioned my final block. A last bit of patchwork and I stood arro-gantly next to my fabulous igloo. 'Tada! Here's one I made earlier.'

Each man sternly inspected my craftsmanship. They sub-jected my palace to rigorous treatment of poking, stamping and shaking. It effortlessly sailed past their stiff examination. Miki proudly presented me the house number sixty-six.

# CHAPTER 12

## Father Knows Best

You may look at what I've done as running away. Everyone is entitled to their own opinion. But it's my life, not yours, and how I choose to live it is entirely my choice. So, take your ideas, expectation, disapproval and general awful attitude, roll them into a massive sphere and shove them somewhere out of sight. Wow! Where did that come from? Forgive me. A fortnight had gone by since my forced exile. And life as an Eskimo couldn't be . . . gosh darn it one day I'll get it right. Life as an Inuit I'd taken a liking to. The language barrier wasn't an obstacle anymore; we sort of meet halfway. I improved their English as they did the same for my Inuktitut. Also, those pathetic hunting days were long forgotten. I now killed with the best of them, including Miki. I filled my extravagant igloo with certain memorabilia; a whale's tail, walrus tusks and slept on a polar bear bedspread. My favourite animal to pursue was reindeer. I'm unsure as to why. There was a location where they congregated, quenching their thirst in parts of the lake that weren't frozen over.

I'd keep my back pressed against the tree and then delicately advance, stalking the weakest one out their pack. His vulnerable little antlers twitched as he lapped up the water. His partners continuously pivoted their heads just in case something looked or smelt funky. He didn't though; the foolish animal gobbled down all his body would permit. I salivated, ogling the poor son of a reindeer. I knew the more liquid he took on board the slower he'd be.

'Just keep drinking, guy; hydration is vital,' I whispered, fetching out a special arrow dipped in a mixture of poisonous plants. I crouched, maintaining my visual, then loaded my bow and pinpointed the feeble target.

He eventually lifted his head and in a split second I released the arrow. My accuracy was unquestionable; I began celebrating before I even connected. The doomed reindeer's scrawny legs quavered, and his pupils narrowed to the size of a grain of sand. He went cross-eyed viewing the arrow of death. His chums scattered like pigeons when a vehicle is approaching. My straight line shot brutally lodged in his skull; blood splatted, making ripples in the lake.

'Booyah!' I exclaimed.

The reindeer jumped out his hooves, a ghastly yelping sound escaped, and he flopped to the ground convulsing.

I nabbed myself another trophy, dragging my kill back to the locals. This manual labour had a profound effect on my stamina and muscular definition. Hauling these three-hundred-pound brutes around promoted muscle growth in ways the gym only dreamt of. In camp my Inuit family applauded as the reindeer's carcass trailed.

'We shall call you "the hunter of deer",' christened Miki.

Miki's wife Yura expertly skinned the reindeer; she brushed the fur using a brush comprised of walrus whiskers. 'Good strong material. I'll get a couple of hats, maybe even a skirt,' she gushed. No word of a lie Yura's fashionable know how would put modern day designer to shame.

Whilst she knitted, clamped and beaded my mind drifted to a life once lived. Was Christmas now formally cancelled? Would December 25th be considered the night Santa forgot?

Although I acted Inuit, partially spoke Inuktitut, owned an igloo and wore their conventional attire, deep inside my soul there was an ultimate clause. Claus, clause … did you spot my sensational wordplay?

Nevertheless, majestic pun aside, my former home was in a state of shock. Father saw aggressive animals and irate elves run his son out of town and barely blinked. He closed the curtains to the living room and carried on reading his newspaper. 'Not my problem. Those who can't hear have to feel,' he condemned.

Mother flustered, miserable in my departure. 'He's our child! Go look for him.'

'Child? The boy's virtually forty. He's got it all sussed. I wouldn't want to interfere.'

'I know you don't mean it; you're a big softy,' said mother, snatching keys to a snowmobile.

'What are you doing?' hollered dad, preventing her from exiting.

'If you won't do what's necessary then I will.'

'You'll do no such thing. He'll learn the world doesn't owe him a thing,' said father sternly.

Mother sobbed for her lost son as those pesky reindeer reappeared. They stumbled back to their quarters.

'You're really washing your hands of him. OK, humour me. In your warped mind how does Christmas pan out?'

Father pushed his glasses to the bridge of his nose and ignorantly read his paper. My workshop lay idle for a whole week; the lock rusted over, and the heating system packed up from inactivity. The elves partied like University students tasting their first slice of freedom. Music blared constantly, empty bottles of booze spilled over trash bins and various mysterious ladies visited their home.

Mother doggedly badgered father to reconcile with me morning till night. She pestered him in bed, in the shower, on the bog and somehow in his sleep.

He snapped one night as she protested in his nightmare. 'Fine!'

'Oh goody! He's crossed the forbidden path and is living with the Inuits,' she explained.

'And how would you know?'

I'd handwritten mom a letter a little while after being accepted. I'm a mommy's boy, deal with it.

'Mother's intuition I guess.'

'I'm not talking about him (Oh I'm him now, how disrespectful). I'll do Christmas like always,' declared father, not too unhappy at an unforeseen second run.

Mom chortled. 'Come on, be serious.'

'What's wrong with me? Wasn't too long ago I cruised the sky, as a solo guy, through the heaviest snow and breezes that were mild, supplying gifts to every good child?'

'I'll tell you what; if you still fit your suit go for it,' challenged mother.

It's widely known the Claus men have wild genetics; we are naturally big-boned. Dad amassed a grotesque gut; he'd often rest his dinner plate on it. Don't ask how I'm positive he can't say, but father remarkably squeezed, nudged, lubricated and caressed his obese frame into his suit. 'You were saying?' he boasted as oxygen struggled to reach his brain.

'I've seen leggings with more room.' Mother shook her head in disappointment.

'It works for me. My second stint shall commence,' announced father, wearing his famed hat to hide his face turning a dangerous purple.

'I got a stipulation though. When it dawns on you, you're fighting an uphill battle, you bring our lad home.'

'I'll concur,' he replied, rapidly undressing to prevent blacking out.

By morning father had slipped back into his old pattern, rising before the sun climbed to the sky's summit. He filled his flask with a strong blend of coffee and greased the lock to the workshop. There dad concluded what a mammoth task he'd inherited. 'What a mess!' He fixed the boiler; as age snuck up on him father felt the cold more. As the commotion from the workshop stirred, hung over Hamilton and Fletcher were also roused. The sight of father filing, spraying and glossing rekindled their faith.

'He's back!' yelled Fletcher.

The elves washed and sprinted to his side. He promptly brought them back into the fold. Their half a century partnership instantly bore fruit. They operated almost as one. Each person went above and beyond, comprehending time had them by the short and curlies. No fag breaks, lunches were eaten at desks and yet still they seemed destined to fail. Their relentless charge continued in this vein for six whole days.

'How is it we're not making great strides?' wondered father.

It's long been said you're the last person to know you don't have it anymore. Father's body was exhausted. His joints chronically ached to a point that he now used deep heat as moisturizer. Under his clothes he supported himself with a back brace, patella bands and several metres of injury tape held him together. Dad was falling apart and there was absolutely nothing he could do to alter it. Regardless of whether they met their quota father gauged him delivering on Christmas Day wasn't realistic. He fought hard against his initial pride and then ever so slightly hinted at reinstating me. The elves immediately pooh-poohed the idea, reeling off a lengthy list of reasons as to why I'm not Santa Claus material.

'That's my son you're bashing,' said a mortified father.

'Hey, I call 'em how I see 'em,' responded Fletcher, completing his gift wrapping.

'You guys did everything to undermine him. Look where we are now.'

Fletcher flaked a minute. He didn't retort right away. Instead he paused for thought, rubbing his chin. 'I'm willing to listen to reason.'

Father civilly heard Fletcher's wrangling, finding out what the elves required, preferred and would compromise on. Armed with enough information, he made the daunting walk into Inuit country. I spotted his hobbling old man trot like that. He staggered around Igloo after Igloo, showing embarrassing photos from my childhood. 'Have you seen him?' Dad spoke slowly and loudly. The Inuit community is fiercely loyal they don't rat out one their own. Ultimately father came up sonless and he contemplated leaving. Miki witnessed my body language; he recognized the eager eyes and stopped my father, directing him over.

I retreated into my igloo. Dad followed, getting his bulky torso stuck; his legs dangled outside. I modified my tunnel to comfortably fit two people, so it goes to shows father's retirement physique.

And you thought we fitted through chimneys. Unbelievable.

'Help me out, son.'

I tugged his arms in as Miki shoved his feet. We pushed and thrust, making no inroads.

'He's as snug as a pug. I'll get a shovel,' said Miki.

I didn't wait for father to say his piece. 'I've got a new life now; somewhere I can be me.'

'Look me dead in my eyes and say it.'

He'd given me an out. I locked in, pupil to pupil, but was incapable of setting myself free. A healthy silence dwelled between father and me only interrupted by Miki digging. He tossed snow aside better than a dump truck; soon daylight sneaked around dad's body.

'I'm not returning. Under no circumstance. Xmas isn't ruining my life like yours.'

'Ruined my life?' queried dad, getting looser.

'Christmas is a family holiday, yet every year you were so fatigued you practically slept till mid-January. What a wonderful family tradition.'

Father crawled inside my igloo, sitting on the self-made reindeer chair. 'You think it's easy leaving your family? You honestly believed I wouldn't have rather stayed home? Santa Claus is a thankless task.'

He was making my point for me. 'Precisely, so why bother?'

A pensive look adorned dad's face. He gradually unzipped a black travel bag, deploying his last play to persuade me. 'It's not about us son. It never has been.' Father loaded up his tablet, selecting a couple videos at random. 'This is why.'

The videos weren't of the best quality, but they clearly showed children from the most deprived parts of the planet receiving presents. These kids barely had a pot to you know what in, so this magical time of year helped ease the other three hundred and sixty-four miserable ones.

'Do you really wanna be that guy who destroyed their hope of happiness?'

I wept on my reindeer blanket like a child scolded by their father. 'I've been selfish. I never viewed the bigger picture.'

He tenderly embraced me. 'Come home, son.'

'What about the elves?' I fretted.

'Let's say they've seen the light.'

With father backing me I packed up said my sad good-byes to Miki, Yura and Yuka then we briskly roamed home.

# CHAPTER 13

## His Father's Son

It was the night before Christmas and Santa had no cheer

For this was his most troubling and testing year

Including defiant elves, ruthless reindeer with a mind of their own

On top of a bull-headed father who'd eventually change his tone

Limits were exceeded, boundaries broken

For what remained was a bond unspoken

A heavy laden Moon guarded blissful stars and roads buried in snow

Whilst millions of giddy children speculated whether or not Santa would show

Fletcher and I stayed out of each other's way. He didn't like me, and I despised everything about him. His friends fed off his arrogance. They snapped their fingers whenever they wanted my assistance. For them to agree to my rehiring, I basically conceded on every point. They controlled the workshop, played their favourite jingles, set the room

101

temperature and rearranged our workstations so I now occupied a middle desk. They reckoned it helped integrate us. I knew not to bother bickering; instead I held in my displeasure. Any potential business owners out there, here's some stellar advice. Never let your employees know their true value or else they'll begin to challenge the company that paid them enough to survive, but not live without complaints. You must crush, crumple, humiliate and lower your staff's spirit to nullify an uprising. You won't be liked or loved, which is slightly overrated. What you will gain is monumental power. I can say what I want about Fletcher's corrupt crew, however their one redeeming feature was a tenacious work regimen. We pulled five consecutive all-nighters, grafting tirelessly. With each gift completed Hamilton deleted them off our present indicator. By December 23rd we were within three thousand.

I glanced at the guys, more as co-workers than employees. 'If you were betting men, what odds would give us?'

'Hundred to one,' said Fletcher.

'Geeze, remind me to place a wager at your betting shop,' I responded.

'Me too,' added Hamilton as the digital indicator dropped below three thousand. 'Maybe I'm being generous. I forgot this is Nick Clause.IV, after all. The fourth instalment of a legendary legacy.'

I took his comment as a faint compliment, although I was unsure whether it was said sarcastically. 'What about you lot? The much-esteemed helpers embarking on yet another changing of the guard. Longevity is something to be admired.'

Fletcher smiled and subtly winked. 'Kudos to Santa and the elves.'

# The Night Santa Forgot

As we miraculously clawed ourselves out of the gloom a mutual appreciation transpired between me and the elves. Behind the sinister barbs they were awfully nice people and very hard workers. I saw why my great-grandfather originally hired them. At midday on Christmas Eve the gift monitor switched into double digits. Although our goals were actually achievable energy reserves were depleted. The elves operated on instinct; thank goodness they could manufacture toys in their sleep. I amazingly observed them sleepwalking while cutting wrapping paper to the correct length. To prevent myself dozing I tied my hair tightly, tugging at the roots. The excruciating pain kept me awake. Father insisted on lending his expertise upon visiting the chaotic workshop. His sheer presence galvanized us. We summoned up every fibre of willpower and surged through the final ninety items. Dad fittingly lay the last piece of Sellotape.

'Get in there, my son,' squealed Fletcher.

A real air of accomplishment prevailed. Sadly, nobody had the liveliness to celebrate. Most elves dropped where they stood sleeping like newborns. Roughly I had an hour of dead time to kill before my journey. Father and I shared a cheeky brandy sitting at my new station.

'I know Xmas is in good hands,' he spoke fondly.

'It was in doubt for a while.'

'Nah, you suffered growing pains. It's entirely natural.'

'So, running away is some weird rite of passage?' I questioned.

Father chuckled, exposing his molars which were all silver with fillings. Decades of mince pies, cookies and other treats had corroded his teeth, causing multiple cavities. Great; there's another problem I gotta look forward to. 'If it's any consolation to you, your departure was easily the best. I wound up coming home forty-five minutes into my exit.'

'Wow! Couldn't hack the harsh night?'

'Me and your grandfather had a blazing row over something trivial. Me, thinking I'm all that and a packet of crisps, upped and went. Now imagine this; it's thirty below zero and I'm turning to ice. The North Pole was scarcely populated back then. The elf guesthouse was merely a blueprint and the Inuit families didn't move here until the late seventies. I'd never spent a day outdoors and one gust of unnerving wind took me from Johnny big bananas to a feeble child. I remember jetting home, begging for father to let me in.'

'Incredible. I figured my struggles were unique,' I said, feeling somehow more connected to the Santa Claus moniker than ever.

'Son, please. Your great-grandfather quit four times, twice on the same night. My dad himself headed for the border on Christmas Eve of all days. Say, lad, I'd have been worried if you'd sailed through the Father Christmas process unscathed.'

'So you wanted me to fail?'

Father came in closer; he tilted the bottle, pouring out a double brandy for himself. 'What happened wasn't failing. You, my boy, graduated.'

We drank to my success. He reminisced about some of his own burdens. In my thirty odd years of being my father's son he'd never spoke so freely. I enjoyed this person's company; his charisma delighted me. The insight he bestowed would serve me a lifetime and serve my children and grandchildren too. It was one of those occasions I wished lasted forever. Unfortunately, a deafening bell rang out; its metal clapper consistently clattered against the bell's outer shell. The bell had a timer fitted which signalled a setting sun in Fiji. Why Fiji? Fabulous question; remind me to put additional socks in your stocking. With varying time differences across the world Fiji will be the first place to celebrate Christmas, hence why I kept tabs on their current local time.

A meteoric silence lingered inside the workshop father and I knew what was to come.

Before we muttered any words, mother galloped through the doors clutching my dry cleaned Santa suit. She slipped it out the packaging, shoving it into my chest. 'Take a whiff son, no trace of Jeremy's juice. Dry cleaners threw in a deep steam once they discovered who it was for.'

'You heard the lady, children are calling,' said father, getting rather choked up, his voiced withering.

Faster than a flash of lightning I suited up as Fletcher and Hamilton loaded my sleigh. They were masterful stackers; how they fitted over one billion toys on a sleigh beggared belief. Once the sleigh was fully stocked there wasn't much else to say. Mother and father wandered out to the runway, waiting to wish me off. I had a lingering gander around the barren workshop. Stations were garnished with sweat, screwed up energy bars and many heart-warming memories. I settled my emotions, inhaled deeply, tightened my big boy shoes then prepared to unleash Santa Claus IV. I strode not walked (it is important to note that) to where the reindeer were cooped. We weren't chummy but came to an amicable solution. Provided I didn't feed, pet or act aggressively they'd do what was asked. I politely ushered them to the sleigh that lay twenty yards away. Father and I securely fastened each reindeer into their harnesses.

Fletcher gave the sleigh's engine a thorough service. His unibrow marginally rose in a surprised fashion, his nose twitched, and body shivered.

A sudden wave of queasiness erupted in my stomach. Fletcher's unusually expressions were disturbing; he hollered at Hamilton. They both animatedly conversed, trying not to appear rattled.

'What's wrong? Let me in on the convo, I'm flying the darned thing,' I said frowning. I needed a fear of flight like a bucket needs a hole.

'The hell you are,' claimed mother, yanking the keys from the ignition.

'Behave will you, woman. He goes regardless of what mommy says,' confirmed dad.

Mother assertively turned to father; her normal affectionate face was replaced by something from you'd see on Friday 13th.

A subdued father stumbled back in the snow his hands caught his fall.

'Could you live with yourself if catastrophe struck?' she asked, looming over dad.

He gingerly stood up, flicking snow from his hands. 'No, of course not.'

'Its fuel injected, Fletch. A carburetor serves no purpose,' clarified Hamilton.

'That's explains why I couldn't find it.' Fletcher smoothly downplayed his error.

'She's all yours! Primed, prepped and full of beans,' he grinned.

For those remotely interested, a carburetor combines fuel and air for internal combustion engines. Whereas fuel injection engines pump fuel directly into the engine. See? I educate as well as entertain.

The reindeer jolted slightly, anxious to get going. The longer I prolonged take-off their core temperature cooled, increasing the risk of injury. 'Guess I'll see you when I see you.'

Hamilton and Fletcher saluted me.

Mother waltzed to my sleigh, bombarding me with a million kisses. 'Have a safe journey.'

As I went to input the first home in Fiji father pinched my wrist.

'You won't get far without this son,' he informed, clasping a gold chain around my neck. At the end of the chunky gold links dwelled a key.

'Really? For me? And I didn't get you anything,' I joked.

He delicately slapped me on my forehead. Parents suggest they're love taps but I prefer to think of them as child abuse. 'Funny one, you are. That there's your master, the only one in existence. It'll morph to open any front door you desire.'

'Stupid! Stupid! How could I forget?' I said cursing myself.

'Give yourself a break. You were already spinning too many plates. Now go give them hell son,' he encouraged, stepping back.

I sat in the driver's seat, straightened my hat as the clearest of nights presented itself starless, cloudless with a radiant full moon making visibility perfect. A light tug of the reindeer's straps and we hurried down the runway. Having suffered a terrible flying encounter for not following father's instructions first go round I adopted his favourable strategy of counting the reindeer's strides. When they shortened to two per second, I ignited the engine. Its boisterous rumble shocked the reindeer, who were used to the softer motors of previous sleighs. The twin propellers frenetically rotated, gaining maximum intensity. We glided to the runway's apex, displacing tons of snow. As significant daylight between us and the snow was attained reindeer after reindeer folded their legs towards to their bodies. They were so in tune with who tucked in next it looked a lot like a sky bound bobsled team.

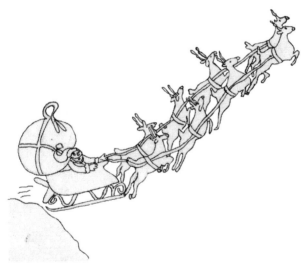

I pinpointed a wonderful flying height above the birds and below the airplanes. Children of Fiji beware; Santa Claus is coming to town.

# CHAPTER 14

## Delivering the Goods

They say it's not how you start but how you finish. I'm living proof. Never in my wildest dreams did I fathom this Santa suit fitting me so well. It felt natural, as if I'd been Father Claus since birth. We drifted through the sky like carefree birds exploring new destinations. My sleigh was a sturdy one; not a single toy budged. The reindeer quietly coasted upfront without grunt, groan or moan. The humming engine behind me never sounded so sweet.

My visual landmarks told me we hovered over the South Pacific Ocean. As midnight approached Fiji so did I. Now Fiji's an independent Island in Melanesia hosting around a million people. Some aren't kids and they're not on my list. Neither were a lot of children and it wasn't because of their ghastly behaviour. By all account several counties were completely no-go zones. Vietnam, Somalia, Laos, Cambodia, Kuwait, Uzbekistan, Iraq, China, Congo, Algeria, Yemen, Kazakhstan, United Arab Emirates, Libya, Iran, Azerbaijan, Comoros, Oman, Mongolia, Turkmenistan, Bhutan, Nepal,

North Korea, Qatar, Saudi Arabia, Mauritania, Tajikistan, Bahrain, Israel, Tunisia, Afghanistan, Morocco, Thailand, Turkey and the Maldives all declined Crimbo. Then there's Russia who, celebrate Christmas on January 7th. Don't squirm, Russian children, thinking oh me oh my, he missed us. I'll be back. One reason in particular certain regions shun Christmas is down to religious beliefs. Let me say from my heart to yours happy Hanukkah and Kwanzaa.

As the sleigh bells jingled and jangled, warning others of our descent, I scanned for a quiet location to park up. Scouring Fiji's capital of Suva, I identified a fantastic landing strip. Touching down in a sleigh rammed out with numerous presents challenged me to the utmost. One false move and we'd topple being squashed under 3.2 tons of toys. My decelerating sleigh informed the reindeer, who promptly released their legs. I yanked the reins, swerving us past homes high in the hills. Alive and well, we landed on a grassy embankment above the soothing ocean. The reindeer's antlers flailed, impressed by my landing abilities. I unhitched myself from these restricting safety features mother insisted on, collecting my first gift.

The home rested on uneven turf; builders added wooden stumps to stabilise it. From the looks of things this country was predominately penniless. Most roads were dirt based and I couldn't see a lamppost for love nor money. Had it not been for my sleigh's headlights I'd have been consumed in blackness. Huts comprised of wooden beams; many were roofed by thin straw or hay. They weren't spread out in an ideal way either, being far too close or acres apart. Whoever designed the layout needs a swift kick. Nonetheless, I scooped the present under my armpit before walking briskly towards the door. The nearer I got my right palm itched, becoming hotter, and by the time stepped on their porch a sizzling sensation had begun. Panicking, I peered down, viewing a true Christmas miracle. Father's master key fizzed, its original flat shape transforming into a sharp edge adapting itself for a new lock. Without me having to wriggle it, the key effortlessly slotted into the lock. I carefully twisted the handle, tiptoeing inside. Beyond the average exterior dwelled an equally mediocre interior. All the furniture was hand-crafted from wood, the walls consisted of dried mud and no carpet covered floors; instead, rough straw resided there. If I'd known sooner, I'd have weaved them a reindeer rug. Sorry, that's the Inuit in me talking. As for entertainment, a black and white T.V rested on a wonky wooden stool. I knew of poverty but not to this extent. The family was so hard up their daughter didn't ask for a typical doll house, Easy-Bake Oven or cuddly toys. No-no, she used her freebie on a solar powered lantern. Fiji nights can get ridiculously dark, as though someone took a black permanent marker to the sky. In her situation the lantern had two functions; in the evening it saved her parents electricity and at night eased her concerns. I popped the box under their tree and set out to deliver Fiji's remaining 87,943 presents.

We hit the Pacific Ocean harder than merciless fighter jets. Except all we spread is love not toxic bombs. I also conducted business in the more established countries of Australia and New Zealand. That's where I got my helpings of mince pies and cream. This is one thing I recall from father's Christmas travels; he'd often bring home a variety of strange puddings for our sampling. It seemed like every country had their specialities. The reindeer received carrots, celery and a handful of sprouts; no doubt left by some cunning children. They munched away, crunching on the hard texture. I tipped a little water into silver bowls to support their digestion. This meant I broke a rule they stipulated of no feeding. Apprehensively I slid a bowl under their chins, expecting to be speared. Surprisingly each reindeer gladly gulped down the water at will. Were they starting to find my charm irresistible? I brazenly patted one their coats, testing our newfound understanding. The reindeer's short furry tails swayed in excitement. No one human, animal or alien should ever hold grudges. Grudges fester, producing a spiteful, bitter and evil version of you. I was content in letting the past be the past.

The Middle East and Asia is probably Santa's easiest stretch; I barely left my sleigh. We blitzed an entire continent over a three-hour span. Gifts were flying off my sleigh like ripened apples off trees. The half-ton weight loss I underwent allowed me to tickle the accelerator. You don't buy a highly tuned turbo-boosted sleigh for comfort and reliability, do you? I put the sky on notice, searing through clouds as if competing in a Red Bull Air Race. Extremely enthralled, the reindeer giggled loudly, if reindeer are capably of giggling. My sleigh's tenacious speed gave me a real-life gut check. On frequent occasions I spewed up mince pies. Some of the blowback hit me square in the mush. Yuck! Yucky! Yuckier!

My aerial madness had us in Africa, where I drank some Magnesia mother supplied knowing I got travel sick from time to time. Africa has a somewhat abnormal fascination with seconds not the time, more the rankings. It's the world's second biggest continent after Asia and secondly, it's second in population behind Asia too. So far, my trip had revealed new cultures, new countries, new animals and new tribes. Tribal families in Africa were more common than I anticipated. We rocked into the West African country of Nigeria and a hot sweltering night met us at the border. Amongst Nigeria's sophisticated cities lived shanty towns you wouldn't see on a holiday brochure. Raw sewage littered the streets. Gaunt stray dogs rummaged trash heaps and disillusioned goats couldn't muster up enough self-worth to dispose of bloodsucking flies. Busted homes with sheets for walls, unwanted plants growing in the living room and cardboard doors housed families of six. These images deeply sadden me.

However, the reindeer appeared desensitised. They'd seen wretched poverty every twelve months so thought nothing of it.

'What a wonderful world we live in,' I said, crestfallen.

My master key was a useless object here. I peeled away the duct tape, leaning the cardboard door against its frame.

In their home a harrowing sight broke my heart further. Six kids lay top to tail in one bed. They were like tinned mackerel, so confined and compressed. Their parents, Mr and Mrs Cisse, slept standing up and if it's a fraction as uncomfortable as it looked then they're in for some serious spinal issues. They grimaced while snoring. The Cisses brought their children up with the best intentions: dignity, manners and a wealth of love. Their kids were another bunch who stuck out on my list for noble reasons. The presents they requested weren't self-serving gifts either. The Cisses' eldest son asked for a bicycle with a basket, so he could ride the six miles to a well filling a pail full of clean water. He'd recently witnessed his mother faint carrying a heavy bucket placed on her head. His sisters decided to surrender their individual gifts, hoping I'd grant Mr and Mrs Cisse a double bed. Lastly their baby brother, following his older siblings' examples, sought a lawnmower with the ambition of him and his father starting a lawn mowing service. And I respected that more than anything. I obliged them all. Upon reviewing their kid's letters to Santa the Cisses were astonished as well as mortified. Are we bad parents? They thought privately. Rather than toys and gadgets their offspring seek household items. To make themselves feel less like failures Mr and Mrs Cisse scrambled enough fabric to sew me a customary dashiki. Dashikis are V-neck pullover garments that are commonplace in western Africa for males. The bright colours genuinely complemented my blue eyes and it being loose fitting meant my stomach had room for expansion. I cherished my dashiki, wearing it casually around the North Pole.

I swept through Africa like a Tsunami, minus the mass devastation and countless casualties. Just substitute that with exceptional joy and abundant happiness. I'd completed three out of six continents. Now before you brainboxes get on my cases announcing there are seven continents, dummy, do you know anyone who lives in Antarctica? Well neither do I. We organised ourselves for the dire European leg. If the Middle East and Asia were the starters, then Europe was definitely the main course. Two thirds of my deliveries were on this continent; the continuous stop and go motion of my sleigh interrupted our flow. Add to that Europe's harsh winters, the fact my feet were blistering from walking up and down driveways, the reindeer gasped for oxygen whenever we landed plus tiredness set in for all parties. I tackled Belarus, dispatching gifts in a robotic trance: open door, leave present then depart. Open door, leave present then depart. Deliveries lost their oomph; at some stage I began dumping presents on doorsteps, ringing the doorbell and shooting off. When I hopped in the sleigh, totally spent, I sagged noticing my G.P.S displaying directions for Finland.

'Oh goody,' I huffed.

After our spat, the Finnish people branded me public enemy no.1. Parents spoke freely about their disdain towards me on www.I hate Santa Claus and here's why?.com. I'm starting to believe the internet was exclusively created for trolling. I replied to a few scathing comments, only fuelling more hatred. A sadistic streak in me wanted to sabotage Finland's Christmas by missing them entirely. But I'm not that kind of guy. As I homed in on Helsinki, a snowy blizzard gave us whats for, cascading snow from all angles. Don't be concerned, we weathered it. Once the stormy element passed, I efficiently distributed what was needed. A lot of homes boycotted the customary mince pies. Can't say I'm bothered. The reindeer and I kept a formidable pace along the Finnish countryside as snow hindered my vision. By and large a white sky mirrored the ground it paralleled, except for a dazzling star. The twinkling sky diamond enticed me. What is it with me and stars? I pursued it just like before, never letting a cloud come between us. Not too long down the line the star emerged shinier, bolder and superior, perched over a narrow, terraced home. Quickly I made an abrupt stop; the reindeer's hooves skidded to a standstill on hazardous black ice. Upstairs a little boy hid behind his curtain; I saw the material rustle as he peeked. This home engrossed me in untold ways. My brain was so obsessed I forgot the gift. I unlocked the door, still unaware of its significance. In the lounge next to three stockings hung above the fireplace lay two giant toffee and fudge cookies accompanied by a glass of milk. As I gobbled away a quiet but distinct plodding noise gained momentum. From out the landing area a sleepy-headed child yawned; his face was as elated as if seeing Father Claus on Christmas morning. Which in fact he was. I squinted, recognising his freckly cheeks and grimy hands.

'Santa!' he went to yell, then remembered he should be sleeping and muted his volume.

'Jeremy! Merry Christmas,' I said merrily.

'I thought you weren't coming. You were furious last time we spoke.'

I crouched near Jeremy, putting one arm on his shoulder more for balance than sincerity. 'Father Claus overreacted that night. I was wrong and I hope you accept my deepest apologies.'

We shared a friendly hug.

'Now didn't you order a drone, Jeremy?'

He energetically nodded.

Shall we see what I got in my sleigh?'

'Oh please,' he squealed.

Jeremy and I roamed to the sleigh. He stroked the reindeer while I fished out his gift.

'Here we are, lad. Now don't say I didn't bring you anything.'

'Thanks Santa. I'll never leave negative posts about you again.'

'Good to know.'

A jubilant Jeremy sprinted indoors out of the wintery snowstorm. I however battled the big freeze; my nose tip turned a poignant red. Reindeer snivelled; tears tenderly trickled off their faces and mine too. We all liked to imagine it is Randolph's elaborate humour, displaying he knows what's happening.

Buoyed that we had aired our grievances, I demolished Europe like the iceberg did the Titanic. Simply forget the sinking feeling and exchange it for high spirits. Not my best scenario to draw comparisons from, I'll agree. I breathtakingly romped through Italy, France, Sweden, Germany and

England on the European back stretch. The final instalments took me to the terrific setting of South America; vibrant beats and carnival atmospheres were almost universal. I scattered my gifts across Chile to Mexico. Then I concluded business in North America pleasantly upbeat and, for the first time in a long time, happy to be heading home.

# CHAPTER 15

## Christmas with the Clauses

Situations in life have a peculiar way of looking their darkest before doing a marvellous 180. Who'd 've thunk it; me fantasising about next year's adventure. Yet here I am planning shorter routes to shave time off my journey. I brought us home a minute shy of noon, planting us on a platform next to our workshop. In unshackling the reindeer, they wearily slumped to their huts, sleeping till sundown. My sleigh's engine vibrated as multiple fans attempted to cool down its frenzied overheating. The motor rustled and smoked for hours as the savage temperature gradually reduced. The sleigh served me well considering it travelled around the world in under twenty-four hours. And a book would have you believe it'd take you eighty days. Seriously? A profound stench of burning oil engulfed the North Pole. The smell conjured up fond memories of father re-joining us on Christmas morning. I snorted in the foul odour like I was using a nasal inhaler.

'Could this be any more Christmassy?' I asked for a moment.

It's good to relax knowing I've got three hundred sixty-four days until the frustration, strenuous work and tiresome slog unfolds again. What was to come bear no mind because as soon as I waltzed into my home mother's cooking controlled my thoughts. A delicious roast turkey glistened in the oven; mom drizzled oil to keep the breasts moist. Jackie, her daughters and Terrell's wife were assisting mother every step of the way. Terrell, his disorderly boys, the elves and papa reclined, chomping on cheese nibbles and downing pale ale. Save your complaints saying we're sexist. We alternate culinary duties yearly, and this time it was the girls.

'Hey guys, crimbo can officially commence,' I said, hanging up my Santa suit.

I heard pots and pans clatter against the sink as three enchanted little girls came dashing over.

'Uncle Nicholas,' exclaimed Anna.

'Santa Claus,' squealed her sister, correcting her.

'Father Uncle Claus Nicholas,' said their middle sister, confused about what to call me.

'I gather Christmas is going well,' I replied, savvy to their answer.

'Absolutely! You outdid last year's gift giver,' declared Anna.

'Oi, I heard that,' bellowed father in a peeved tone.

'Sorry Granddad.'

Father prised himself off the couch, lurching into the hallway. 'So long as I'm your favourite grandparent I'll let the last statement slide.'

Anna innocently shrugged. 'Sure, why not, let's go with that.'

120

'Girls, I've got parsnips and carrots that require peeling and washing,' shouted Jackie.

The three girls zipped off to the kitchen, their pigtails swaying from side to side.

A magnificent glimmer bedazzled dad's pupils when he gazed at me. His admiration was difficult for him to contain. He couldn't decide whether to hug or shake hands. 'Proudest moment of my life seeing you take to the sky.'

'I'm told it's in the genes; us Claus men have the Christmas fire in our bellies,' I said passionately.

Father clutched his chest, all choked up. He seemed emotionally overwhelmed at how I'd developed. 'No more beautiful line has ever been spoken. Don't keep me in suspense lad, how was it?'

'To sum up my experience in four words: exhausting but worth it,' I explained, forcing off my boots and sitting on the bottom stair.

By this time Fletcher and Hamilton joined the reunion, praising my debut outing. 'Knew you had it in ya,' they commended.

'Look at those blisters. You wanna soak them boy, then use an Aloe Vera foot cream before wrapping them in clingfilm at bedtime,' dad advised. 'Noted. I'll do it immediately.'

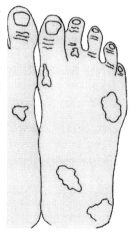

'Slow your role, kidda. We want vivid details of Santa's great adventure,' stated Fletcher.

Our lounge area was awash with people; elves occupied the couches and stools. Terrell's bothersome

121

children were sitting two inches from the TV whilst Terrell himself slouched across an entire three-piece sofa. My entrance ushered a silence not seen before or since. Everyone ceased motion like when the music stops in musical statues.

I arrogantly sauntered in, nudging Terrell's foot. 'Budge up T, I got a story to tell.'

His face fumed, anger emitted through the eyes, pulsating nostrils and his constant chewing of his bottom lip. 'Sure, there you go bro,' he snarled.

I divulged my exceptional escapade to a spellbound audience. Father, the elves, Jackie's awkwardly shy husband, even Terrell's brats remained riveted. They gripped cushions, mugs, ornaments, anything they could find. Their excitement only distanced me and Terrell further. He cursed my every line and refuted my boastful claims. I talked for England that afternoon, not missing out a single event. I spoke until those brilliant words we all long to hear on Christmas Day.

'Dinner is served.'

A Claus Christmas is nothing to sneeze at; we do it to the fullest. Mother's a prime example. As far as I go back, she'd set out Twelve Drummers Drumming, Eleven Pipers Piping, Ten Lords a-Leaping, Nine Ladies Dancing, Eight Maids a-Milking, Seven Swans a-Swimming, Six Geese a-Laying, Five Gold Rings, Four Calling Birds, Three French Hens, Two Turtle Doves and A Partridge in a Pear Tree sculptures representing the twelve nights of Christmas. I couldn't ever tell if father actually gave two hoots about the ornaments; all in all, he placed them on the coffee table.

We hurried out the living room like a team of inspired footballer players after a halftime pep talk. Father led the starving bunch. Mother patrolled the dining room, pointing to who sat where. Upon entering I noticed she'd laid out an additional place mat and cutlery set. Mother was very astute woman; nothing got by her observant mind. Trust me, as children we were under lock and key.

The family shoved their chairs forward under the table. Terrell and Jackie's kids tucked their napkins into their tops. All food lovers made lust-filled advances towards the sizzling feast.

Mother slapped hands, prising away forks. 'Nobody start consuming. We're one guest short.'

Everyone stared at the person to their right, left then opposite.

'Are you going senile love? Everybody's present,' said Father.

People began wondering who'd be the mystery attendee. They threw out random names. 'David Beckham?'

'Cold,' said Mother.

'Victoria Beckham?'

'I'd have thought the Beckhams spend Christmas together,' responded mom.

Anna and her sisters tried an intelligent process of elimination using their family tree. 'It's our great uncle Giovanni,' they figured.

'Safe to say it's not him, pet,' mother whispered.

Uncle Giovanni's ashes were in an urn atop the mantelpiece.

'All will be revealed.'

Then suddenly a rattle resonated as the steel knocker peppered our door. 'You should get that son,' dryly grinned mom.

'What you been up to lady?' I probed.

She stayed tight lipped just harmlessly swigging her Chardonnay.

I had a sneaky inclination as to who it might be and desperately combed my hair and doused myself in aftershave. The assumption was dead on as, standing there in a flawless gown, stood Molly looking ravishing. In letting her inside I got queasiness in my tummy the likes you get when you're sick. Santa had a bad case of the love bug.

Mother had taken it upon herself to play cupid she sent a D.M inviting Molly to a "Claustatic Christmas". Her words not mine. Mothers: you show them how to operate a computer and now she's Bill Gates. We hadn't been on a first date and Molly's spending Xmas with the folks. I sheepishly introduced her as a close friend.

'She's here, can we please eat?' asked dad.

'Nick Jnr. carve that bird,' instructed mother, passing around a bowl of cheese and chive infused mash potatoes.

The golden-brown turkey nestled on a silver platter. Steam rose off its succulent flesh. Terrell's eager kids banged their knives and forks against the table. Sparks jumped off my knife when sharpened it. I stabbed the bulky bird with a carving fork; transparent juices oozed out its crispy skin, a clear indication of it being properly cooked. I sliced the bird evenly, ensuring Terrell received a crusty drumstick. He hissed and mumbled, shaking his head. I smirked, feeling I'd got one over on him. Aware his sons were at loggerheads Father frowned, although with his crumpled face who knew?

We said grace, pulled Christmas crackers and put in work. Plates quaked under masses of roast spuds in goose fat, honey roasted vegetables, luscious turkey, pigs in blankets, an almond and pecan stuffing, cranberry sauce and ungodly boiled sprouts drenched in Mom's special gravy comprising of ... Unfortunately, I'm sworn to secrecy. We ate until we all resembled patients on a maternity ward. I popped my top button, getting the meat sweats. After exercising our jaw muscles rigorously, the ladies retired, leaving us men to tidy up.

Mother was infatuated with Molly; she discovered facts I wasn't aware of. She also had a tendency to embarrass me as displayed here. They chilled in the conservatory admiring the snowy mountains lingering beyond my workshop. 'Nick as a baby was absolutely adorable. I could have gobbled him up on sight.'

Not too horrendous, right? Give her time.

'When it came to breastfeeding, he wouldn't latch on. And when he finally did he bit like crazy.' Mother made an inappropriate hand gesture in case her explanation didn't register.

Oh, how I miss my Inuit life.

Mom persisted, fetching an old childhood scrapbook and recalling the stories behind each disastrous photo. Her extravagant re-enactments had Molly laughing in fits. Every once in a while, Molly caught my eye, and her smiles grew broader. Perhaps mother's make great wingwomen. I mean, who knows more about you than the people who raise you?

With full bellies and love in our hearts, we converged on the living room to swap gifts. Due to my career there's a rule which stipulates I'm exempt from giving presents but happy to collect.

'I'll go first,' said father brashly.

The most cost-effective way of purchasing gifts is a Secret Santa. Dad drew mine and Terrell's name out a hat.

'To my boys with lots of love,' he teased.

Sparkling gold wrapping paper concealed a box. Terrell's eyebrow elevated and curved at the end, as did mine. Instantly our hearts thumped, palms got damp and mouths were parched. Quickly we both discarded its gift wrapper. I felt like I'd been teleported to Christmas 1989. The buzzing excitement had returned.

'Holy smokes, a Sega Genesis,' skipped Terrell.

His kids were unmoved by his antics. 'What's one of them?'

'It's perfect, dad,' I said gratefully.

Now you two behave,' he responded.

'Sonic the Hedgehog or Mortal Kombat?' offered Terrell.

'I have no problem whipping you at both.'

We scurried off upstairs, plugging in the console and nattering like bosom buddies.

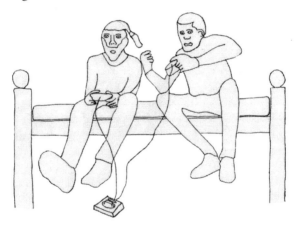

Us Clauses argue, bicker and have lengthy spells of dysfunction but eventually reconcile. I've got no recollection of how the rest of the night unfolded as Terrell and I played until mother confiscated the toy.

'That's unfair mom, I'm an adult,' I protested.

126

'You can get it back in the morning. Now come have some dessert,' she commanded.

'Fine, gosh,' I said mardily.

'You're not too big for a good hiding, son. Molly is your guest and you've barely muttered a word to her. Act like a gentleman; she's a superb girl and passes the in-law examination.'

With that said, Molly and I went off by ourselves. I wowed Molly showing her around her soon to be home. Nothing I divulged scared her away, from my manic work schedule to the sacrifices she'd be expected to make. Molly embraced it all; elves took to her like bread to butter. We ended up talking the night away as the moonlight bloomed in the distance. Molly's snorting laugh was endearing; she wore her waist length brown hair in a scrunchie. I never noticed before her curled eyelashes or the way she struggled pronouncing Rs. My eyes gravitated to hers. My ears carefully processed her words. It's a special sensation when someone gets you. I'm coming off like a lovesick puppy, aren't I? All the same, we arrived outside my workshop. She shivered not use to the North Pole's potent winters I threw my jacket over shoulders.

'Thank you,' said Molly.

'What are friends for?' I replied smoothly.

It was just after midnight, the elves were limping home full of grub. Molly and I watched them staggering, patting their bloated stomachs in hysterics.

'That's final. New year's resolution we're on diets,' proclaimed Hamilton.

'Yeah, I've heard that before,' I yelled.

We stumbled into a casual silence as if we'd run out of interesting talking points. Then our eyes drifted north, glimpsing a huge couldn't miss size mistletoe dangling above the door. Molly's nonchalant attitude was difficult to read. She closed her eyes, tilted her head with puckered freshly coated red lips. I assertively dipped her as we smooched. There we shared true love's first kiss.

'Whitwooooooooooooooooooooooooooooooooooooo!' hollered the elves.

'Alright you perverts cut it out,' I snarled.

Well, from my point of view that's everything. So, if I don't see you beforehand have a happy new year.

I hope you've enjoyed my behind the scenes sneak peek at Santa's world. Thanks for reading and we'll catch up another time.

Printed in Great Britain
by Amazon

67273579R00077